I0741748

The Secret of the Cylinder

Michele Fontaine

The Secret of the Cylinder

Also by Michele Fontaine

Body of Work—Short Stories, Tall Tales, Inspiration,
Wadjet Publishing, 2008.

*Harem Sister—A Young Woman's Quest for Personal Power in Ancient
Persia.* (Book 1 of the *The Sekhmet Series*), Wadjet Publishing, 2001.

Fire of Isis—The Forbidden Temple of Basra. (Book 2 of *The Sekhmet
Series*), Wadjet Publishing, 2002.

"Andean Shamanism Through Wiccan Eyes"
(Shaman's Drum Magazine, Issue #57, January 2001).

"Harem Sister Hits the Road—A Tale of Skukes and Swamp
Yankees" Published on Left Coast Writers' Road Work page, 2003.

"Once Felt, Never Forgotten—On the Road to Bhakti...A
Pilgrimage to the Virgin of Guadelupe in Mexico City" (Indie
Shaman Magazine, London, Issue 17, Summer 2013).

"The Cosmic Dynamo—A New Toltec Teaching Revealed for the
Sixth Sun" (Indie Shaman Magazine, Issue 16, Spring 2013).

"Hot Fudge—A Growing Obsession" San Francisco Chronicle
Food Magazine "My Word" page, January 30, 2005.

"On the Road to Carnal Knowledge" featured in Travelers' Tales
*The Thong Also Rises—Further Misadventures from Funny Women on
the Road,* December 2005.

The Secret of the Cylinder

The Secret of the Cylinder

THE CYLINDER. Copyright© 2015 by Michele Fontaine. All rights reserved. Printed in the United States of America. No part of this book may be used or reproduced in any manner whatsoever without written permission except in the case of brief quotations embodied in critical articles or reviews. For information, contact Wadjet Publishing, 253 Molimo Drive, San Francisco, CA 94927.

Wadjet Publishing is a DBA registered with the County of San Francisco, California, USA.

For information on other publications by Wadjet, as well as ordering information, please contact Wadjet Publishing:
Phone: (415) 530-8391
Email: MBFontaine@aol.com
Web site: www.MicheleFontaine.com

Distributed through IngramSpark.
Available for wholesale acquisition through Ingram and retail through Amazon.com.

Cover design concept, graphic design and book production by Michele Fontaine.

ISBN 978-0-9755207-2-7

Table of Contents.

The Secret of the Cylinder.

Table of Contents.

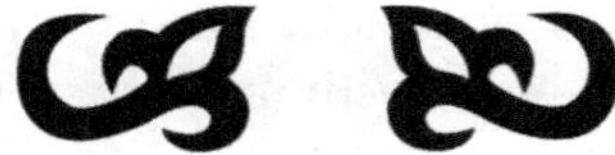

Introduction

Because the telling of a story exists only in community, I am deeply indebted to the many people who have supported the arc of this third novel. Thank you, Dr. Daniel Sadigh for your descriptions of daytime discos in Tehran in the late 1970's as well as other firsthand experiences there. Thank you Farzan Athari for your enthusiasm about my original screenplay version of this book, and for your interest in playing the role of Belshazaar in the upcoming movie.

Thank you, Bill Boyle, for your UCLA screenwriting class and Meetup group, where I learned the unique differences between screenplay and novel writing. You motivated me to create this third book in the series. I always knew it would be a trilogy!

The Secret of the Cylinder

As an exercise for class, I adapted my first novel, *Harem Sister*, into a screenplay. The page count grew as I tried out new, more visual/visceral methods of storytelling; some of which were unique to screenplay writing.

To my initial dismay, my screenplay Meetup group requested more current-day characters, insisting that dusty ancients wouldn't interest modern-day moviegoers. Their feedback resulted in a 120-page script being pared down to ten good pages to move forward with, after six months of writing.

Much to my delight, I discovered that by adding a modern story layer to my ancient tale, and reincarnating my original characters yet again, new life was breathed into my fictional family. Those "ten good pages" traveled with me from LA to San Francisco where I was determined to reverse-engineer the screenplay into a novel.

A year of writer's block followed, from all the editing, auditing, and striving for marketability that goes with screenwriting, as well as the truncated, haiku-like style that is required to create the technical document called the screenplay. I could only write in shorthand for a while; stretching my creative wings in other new directions with paint and canvas.

Eventually, my writing muse returned, and the roadblocks that I'd perceived as hindering that part of myself disappeared. I realized I am at heart a novelist with my love for flowing, embroidered prose, and that I was at last ready to rework what was a screenplay back into the writing style I love most. The third novel was born!

A big thanks to my younger readers and supporters, for your interest and eager anticipation of this new installment. You give me hope for becoming a beloved elder, in the midst of my not having any "children" other than my cats.

Introduction

Gratitude to my beta readers: Rowena Southard, Greg Fuller, Martin Rushmere, Mark McKenna, and Kaitlyn Gallagher from my writer's group B Street Writers. Also Christina Stiegelmeyer and Tejpal Kaur. Your cheerleading and useful suggestions really helped me shape this book.

And the most heartfelt thanks to my partner Gary and our "kids" Tigger and Lila, whose love, kindness, steady emotional support, and fur therapy has comforted, inspired and grounded me over the years throughout the writing of this trilogy.

San Francisco, CA 2015

Introduction

✥ 1 ✥

Shiraz – Qavam House, Eram Garden

Sunday, 12/31/78

"A world of far more sacred importance that they cannot see for their blindness." ~ Charles de Lint

The mansion glows golden, as if boasting of the precious secret that lies within its depths. Mirrored in a rectangular pool below, the palace's image shimmers slightly with a warm evening breeze. A long, slender waterway stretches away from the pool, swelling every 20 feet into circular wells, like pearls on a watery chain. A Persian Paradise garden surrounds it, bordered by the mansion's white vaulted arches leading the eye into the building. Rising before the facade, mature date palms hang heavy with fruit. The scent of rose and jasmine waft sensuously to the third floor, where in a darkened room, a raven-haired beauty is stealing a national treasure.

Faint disco music, clinking glasses, and revelry filter up to the third floor, where the prominent sound is a slight scratching of glass, as she incises a circle on the side of a display case. Inside the clear box, a 2,500-year-old corncob-sized clay cylinder lies nested on four pins. Pressed into its face appear to be the random scratchings of birds. Lit from beneath, the cylinder glows, seemingly with an energy or intelligence of its own.

The Secret of the Cylinder

Dimmed overheads and a small flashlight in her black-gloved hand provide the only illumination. She completes the circular cut and exhales. Looks around cautiously. Then reaches in and takes the cylinder; placing it gently in a beaded black clutch bag. She snaps it closed; the noise making her jump. Looks around.

In her black cocktail dress, she tiptoes on stockinged feet; one hand holding the clutch, the other, her flashlight and a pair of high, strappy black heels. There is no sound except Donna Summer's throaty voice far below. She nears the room's exit.

An alarm jangles loudly to life.

Gasping, she dashes down a darkened hallway. A door bursts open in the distance. Shouts of men. Cones of flashlight rake the gloom.

She emerges out into the night through a service entrance, where a young man kicks a Vespa into a rumble. Hopping on, she clutches him tightly. With an insect-like drone, the scooter buzzes down the alley.

At the far corner of the mansion, an observer smiles and pumps a fist. Then...

BOOM!

A rush of swirling smoke obscures the retreating scooter. The witness' hand flies to her mouth. "NOOSH!" she wails. She races into the black cloud, coughing. Bends over the lifeless forms. Looks up at the clop of approaching feet. Grabbing the beaded

black bag, she races away in the opposite direction, shielded by the billowing smolder of the booby trap.

A hook-nosed young man with the fire of fundamentalism in his eyes appears, lackey by his side.

"So our efforts were not totally fruitless," he mutters approvingly, inspecting the two prone forms.

"Yes, but it seems we've lost the evidence," whines the other, as he pats down the bodies frantically, then scans the vicinity.

The hook-nosed man shrugs, "In good time, my friend...and our time is very near. We'll get the job done properly next time."

Shiraz – Qavam House, Eram Garden

❦ 2 ❧

London – The British Museum, 2021

The cylinder glows in a glass cube display case atop a white pedestal; one of three in a stark, modern room. At its entrance a small boy and a beautiful, 42-year-old raven-haired Persian woman fidget behind a cordon. A hoard of paparazzi press behind them.

"Grandma was very brave, wasn't she?"

"Yes, Tahji, Grandma IS very brave. And so was Grandpa."

A small knot twists in Yasmeen's stomach. The surging crowd is starting to push against her and Tahj. She squeezes the child's chubby hand protectively.

All those murmuring, expectant voices. Wanting something...from her.

From them.

"Back away, people!"

Guards in black suit jackets and open-collared shirts push the paparazzi gently to the periphery.

The Secret of the Cylinder

"Is that a taser, mom?" Tahj points to the squared-off handle poking out from one of the guards' jackets.

"Yes, sweetie...Stay close."

Tasers? Now? I thought we were past all that...

Yasmeen had a finely-tuned radar for potential violence, and was always suspicious of being the center of attention. Just like her mother, Anoush. *How was Mom ever going to face the throng tomorrow, with her post-traumatic stress disorder?* Yasmeen had failed to convince her to join them even for just this small appearance today.

"Which one did Grandma rescue?" A rapt face framed by dark curls gazes up at her. Grounding her.

"The far one." Yasmeen points to the farthest of the three glass display cases. "The one with the statue in it."

She glances at the nearest guard. He eyes his watch, catches the look of another sentry, then nods to Yasmeen. The cordon is unhitched.

Tahj shoots across the room.

Flashbulbs fire. Journalists advance — inevitable and insistent as hungry locusts — followed by threats of instant expulsion by the guards. The cordon is reattached.

Drawing a deep breath, Yasmeen strides across the gleaming floorboards, heels clicking. She glances at the title of the first display case:

Cyrus Cylinder

(6th Century BC. Considered to be the first declaration of Human Rights.)

passes the second:

Nabonidus Cylinders of Sippar and Ur

(6th Century BC. Belshazaar's father, the King, describes how he repaired three temples in Sippar and a ziggurat in Ur. Belshazaar was predecessor to Cyrus the Great. On one cylinder, Nabonidus hopes that Belshazaar "not commit any cultic mistake".)

and approaches the 5-year-old boy, who is hopping in front of the third case.

"I can't see it!" he whines, arms flapping.

"Here" she boosts him up under his arms to adult-level as she reads the title of the third case:

Cylinder of Amat

(6th Century BC. The story of one woman's search for personal power and the discovery of ultimate power. Commissioned by Belshazaar. Residing here when not on loan.)

The Secret of the Cylinder

Tahj squints at the clay artifact. Behind it is a nine-inch tall clay statue of an ample-hipped woman raising her breasts as if in offering. A tiny heart of carnelian is set just below her right collar bone.

Tahj's chubby forefinger follows the line of chicken scratches on the cylinder; cherub mouth shaping perfect words as he says:

"I was born of the desert, and to the desert I must return. By the time you read my story, my bones will have been ground into grains finer than sand, and scattered to the four wind...AAAHHH!

Yasmeen gasps in horror at the child she has dropped onto the hardwood floor. He looks up at her with the pain of betrayal.

Disapproving glances and a ripple of conversation from the paparrazi.

One of the guards rushes over. "Everything OK, ma'am?"

"Um, fine... Thanks. Just a little clumsy today."

"Of course, ma'am. With what your family's been through, and now all this new publicity...Take your time."

Yasmeen bends over Tahj and smoothes his curls as tears well up in his eyes.

"Tahj honey, mommy is SO sorry!"

She signs heavily. "We need to go now...Sweetie, let's get you some lunch." She leads the snuffling, bewildered boy toward the exit.

The assault of questions and cameras makes her knees weak as she passes the journalists.

"Do you think your mother will be awarded or arrested tomorrow?"

"Is the neglect you just showed the boy something you also grew up with, as a result of your mother's accident?"

"Do think the cylinder really has some kind of special power? Or is this just an international hoax?"

A tight smile is her only statement.

Later, sitting outside on the cold marble steps, Yasmeen turns to Tahj, handing him a hot dog from a nearby vendor.

"So when did YOU learn to read Sumerian? You can't even read English yet in kindergarten."

Tahj shrugs, and takes a big bite of lunch.

Am I losing it, or did the cylinder start to glow right before I dropped him?

She shakes her head.

London - The British Museum, 2021

Must've been the flash of a camera...

❧ 3 ☙

Oslo, Norway, December 9, 2021

With a shaking hand, Anoush dabs lipstick to her mouth. Incongruously celebratory lipstick. Lipstick the color of pomegranates, with the scent of tulips. She stops, staring in the hotel bathroom mirror, not at her mouth but at the rest of the disfigured face that follows her everywhere. She flings the tube at the mirror. The pitched lipstick case skitters around the sink like a crazy beetle as Anoush retreats to the toilet seat. Burying her face in her hands. Bursting into tears.

Yasmeen flies across the suite and rushes in.

"It's OK, mom!"

"No, it's *not*! They don't give the award posthumously. He should be here with me today to receive it! I couldn't have done it without him!"

Yasmeen kneels before the frail, trembling woman.

"Daddy will be with us, Mom. I've been feeling him around us today."

Anoush shakes her head. Sniffs. "I thought you didn't believe in that kind of stuff."

Yasmeen shrugs, "Would you like me to accept the award with you?"

A slow nod.

"Then let's be brave together and honor Dad's memory, tomorrow, OK?"

Another nod.

"Tahji can join us too."

A curly head appears in the doorway. "It'll be OK, Grandma. We'll both hold your hands."

At last, Anoush smiles as she folds the small boy in her arms and buries her face in his hair. Inhaling his sweet baby boy scent, she lets his innocence soothe her internal scars for as long as she can surrender to hope and let go of guilt.

"What would I do without you two?" she marvels as she holds his shoulders at arm's length.

"We're here for you, Mom," Yasmeen says. "And we're here for Dad too."

Oslo, Norway, December 9, 2021

Anoush squeezes her daughter's arm as she crushes her grandson to her again.

"OK, I can do this," she sighs, steeling herself.

Oslo, Norway, December 9, 2021

ೞ 4 ಬ

The Nobel Peace Prize Awards,
December 10, 2021

Hours later, a limping 64-year-old Anoush is flanked by Yasmeen and Tahj as they cross a large stage, approaching a podium. Applause thunders. Cameras flash. Upon an enormous screen behind the dais a slide show plays: images of the cylinder from the British Museum, a young Anoush accepting a diploma, an amateurish shot of a handsome young man with an Elvis hairstyle.

Tahj points to the screen: "Grampa!"

Yasmeen steadies a suddenly wobbly-legged Anoush. They continue toward the podium.

"And for her discovery and safekeeping of the Cylinder of Amat... until the world was ready for its story. Ready for its miracle. Ready for peace...For her bravery, and the sacrifice of her beloved, we award the 2021 Nobel Peace Prize to...Anoush Telebi."

THUNDEROUS APPLAUSE.

Anoush's shaking hand accepts the award on the big screen.

The Secret of the Cylinder

In the audience an elderly hook-nosed man turns to another. His name tag reads SOROUCH ZARE, Department of Antiquities, Tehran Archaeological Museum. Both men wear dark, nondescript suits. Both could easily be dismissed as retired professors...except for the venom in the yellow eyes of the one.

"Some would stay she's a treasonous thief, and deserves the same fate as her...beloved," he sniffs. "Get the job done properly this time, I say."

His friend raises one finger to his lips, never taking his eyes off the dais.

⚅ 5 ⚅

Tehran 1978 – The Start of the Revolution

A German Shepherd lunges at the door of a house in a middle class neighborhood. The inner glass door shatters, raining shards into the entryway. The dog barks and claws maniacally into the grating that separates him from a cringing woman swathed in a black robe and head scarf. Her husband rushes over to her as she collapses in his arms, quaking in terror.

"Ramiz — we're supposed to be safe now!" she wails.

"Habibah, shhhh..." He rocks her, his murmured comfort drowned out by the resonant barks amplified off stone walls.

A shot is fired in the street. The dog's yelp is cut off.

"Got him!" a young rebel shouts as his camouflage-swathed body appears in the doorway, waving an AKM assault rifle triumphantly. He steps over the dog's lifeless form and races away.

A 4-year-old boy rushes past his parents toward the metal screen to view the dog.

Habibah screams, "Get back, Ilan! This might not be over."

Ramiz sighs, "This won't be over for a very long time.

✧ 6 ✧

Daytime Disco - Tuesday, Dec 19, 1978, Tehran

Two young women enter a dance club in the late afternoon.

"Brick House" by the Commodores plays as a solitary couple in mandatory Western discowear dance awkwardly under a glittery silver ball.

"I can't believe I let you talk me into this," Anoush hisses under her breath.

"Relax!" her pretty companion replies, giving her roommate a playful shove. "Go on!"

After practically toppling onto the dance floor Anoush steadies herself. Before her, the plexiglass floor's geometric shapes illuminate alternately in pink, blue, and yellow like an electric heartbeat; oddly alive and pulsating at 4 p.m. Random strobe lights cross the room: pink anemone-like tentacles reaching for the gentle teens and twenty-somethings. Beckoning them into dreams, possibilities...bright futures, that will soon be cruelly cut short.

Anoush feels geeky and out of place among the flow of jersey and sleek heels. She's a little sorry now that she insisted on wearing a

frumpy, flowery, high-necked dress and flats. Her roommate wears a low-cut, lavender, lettuce-edged cocktail dress that clings to Omid's voluptuous figure like a hungry lover. She's already flirting with someone who looks vaguely familiar from school...gazing down with mock coquettishness at her silver platform heels, giggling, bumping shoulders with him playfully.

Anoush spots other, familiar faces making out at little tables off to the side. She had to see it herself to believe it. This other world—an entirely different face of Tehran—the daytime disco.

"Where else are they going to go?" Omid quips, suddenly back by Anoush's side. Anoush jumps and Omid grins and rolls her eyes at her friend's innocent, wide-eyed gaze. "No privacy at home, or anywhere else for that matter..." Anoush shrugs and accepts a Coke from Omid's new admirer.

"Anoush, this is Rezak. Rezak, Anoush."

"Come here often?"

"Um, no." It's actually my first time.

Rezak shrugs and hands a sloe gin fizz to Omid, who gladly returns to flirting with him.

Anoush swirls the ice in her Coke, focusing intently on the cubes, with a sinking feeling. *I'll always be a wallflower.*

She looks up. And then she sees him. HIM. That cute guy from Professor Abbas' History class at the University. Her cheeks flare,

and wouldn't you know it, just then, he turns and their eyes meet. He nods and starts walking over. Her palms sweat. She clutches the glass tighter.

"I'm surprised...but *happy*... to see you here," he says good-naturedly. "I'm Mirza." His Aramis perfume wafts around her; its leather and gardenia notes caressing her seductively.

"Anoush."

"You might want to be careful not to break that glass," he teases, noting her white knuckles.

Crimson steals over her cheeks again.

"My roommate Omid said I was really missing out on something," she murmurs, braver than she feels. With a wave, she takes in the room. "It's my first time here," she stammers.

"You'll really be missing out on something if you don't *dance* with me."

"Um... I can't."

Mirza raises an eyebrow.

"I mean I can't dance. I'm terrible... I mean, I'd love to, but..."

"Just follow me," he says gently as he takes her hand. She surprises herself by letting him lead her onto the dance floor.

Daytime Disco - Tuesday, Dec 19, 1978,

Mirza is graceful on his feet, and Anoush finds herself falling into a natural rhythm with him, as if they've danced before.

Tendrils of her hair fall out of the '70's teacher bun she's wearing. Her face and chest are flushed...she's enjoying herself, much to her surprise.

Omid watches approvingly from the sidelines with her new man.

Then "Last Dance" by Donna Summer starts. Couples draw closer. Embrace.

Anoush stiffens, but Mirza pulls her close. Her body melts into his, seemingly with a will of its own. She takes a deep breath...and as she relaxes, feels the electricity between them. And a surprising, new hunger. She wonders what his lips would feel like on hers. Just as they lock eyes and it seems he might be thinking that same thought, the music quickens, and they're spinning apart again.

Too soon, the song is over. He leads her back to Omid, leaning into her ear, "Would you meet me tomorrow at Hamid's Coffee House near the University?"

"OK!" she stammers with a shy smile.

"I'd really like to get to know you better. Anoush. How about 3 p.m.?"

"OK. I mean, *yes*. I'd love to. See you then!" she says.

Daytime Disco – Tuesday, Dec 19, 1978,

He nods and steps away.

Anoush turns to Omid and they both duck their heads together and squeal.

Mirza sneaks a backward glance and grins, dimpling deeply.

Daytime Disco – Tuesday, Dec 19, 1978,

❧ 7 ☙

Tehran Coffee House

Wednesday, December 20, 1978

Dark wood, tiny windows—this modern coffee house where Mirza asked me to meet him is surprisingly cozy and intimate. I feel safe here. The feeling is private. Clandestine, even. It's late afternoon. Hazy, golden light paints an interior sunset before me. China clinks.

Occasional laughter ripples from University types in Western clothing, and other locals in traditional robes. In a corner, a young man sits, sketching furiously. Pauses from time to time to take a deep drag off his hookah.

I pass through a cloud of apple-scented tobacco smoke.

And spot Mirza.

Mirza.

When I look at him, I feel I've known him forever. Yet why does he makes me so nervous? Model-handsome, with a high forehead, dimples and that Elvis hairstyle...My breath catches, as it always does when I see his face. I'm wearing no makeup; just a ponytail, my thick glasses, and a white, buttoned up oxford cloth shirt. My

"uniform." He said he wanted to get to know me better, so I just dashed here after class as me, not the "disco queen" I was the other day. Ha! Some disco queen... It felt so natural and exciting to dance with him yesterday. Today I feel like my normal, geeky self.

For a heartbeat my vision blurs and suddenly I see him not as a fellow history student, but in elaborately embroidered robes, and surrounded by well-dressed and deferential livery. Rich jewels glitter on his fingers...

And then I am back, completely disoriented; a shaft of sunlight blinding me.

Luckily, he rises from the table, graceful as a panther. He kisses my hand. I'm grateful since I feel ready to black out. I lean against him and he smiles, surprised.

"You look like you could use a little support...are you OK?"

"Yeah... just felt a little dizzy back there."

"I usually have that effect on women," he grins, and leads me to plump red brocade cushions, festooned with gold tassels and piping. Mirza's casual wave to a waiter instantly brings us Turkish coffee that we sip from tiny blue and white patterned cups. An embossed silver tray lies between us on an ornate Persian rug. The tray holds a plate of dates and white, domed cookies that bear geometric designs in relief.

I dive into the details of this lush environment to distract myself from this sudden wave of shyness. I grab a cookie. Take a bite. To

my horror, a moan escapes my lips. I quickly lower the tidbit. A crumble of rich, green, ground pistachio nuts tumble from inside the cookie onto the plate. Suddenly I feel as exposed as the cookie. What to do?

Mirza gazes at me with a grin. He scoops up a pinch of the pistachio crumble, nibbles it and also moans as he kisses his fingertips.

I could die right now.

But, wait! I'm forgetting what I wanted to show him! With a roll of my eyes and an exasperated sigh—*why does he make me feel so many things?*—I pat the library book by my side. Forgetting my embarrassment. Opening it to the page that shows my treasure. I hear its ancient binding crack. I point to the corncob-sized clay cylinder embossed with cuneiform text on the page. The hooves of long-dead horses can no longer bind this secret. How can I possibly get across to him—this really cool guy—how important this ancient treasure is? Nerves and hormones convince me I can.

"Did you find that dusty old tome in the university library?"

"Yes! I had to beg Professor Abbas to take me into the forbidden stacks. He wouldn't discuss the object of my quest, but led me to this book. I've been searching for this connection with the matrifocal side of our history for a while. I think I've found a valid connection to the goddess culture—or at least a more female-friendly one—that existed in the midst of Darius' reign!

Just imagine, Mirza—something like this could be the find of the century! No, the millennia."

The Secret of the Cylinder

In my excitement, I bump the silver tray between us. China plinks and protests. Coffee spills. Mirza jumps and quickly mops up the mess.

"Sorry!"

"It's OK, Anoush."

He sighs and settles onto his cushion again; a worried frown creasing his beautiful brow.

"We both know the Shah's days are numbered and this kind of research right now could put you in danger. Why are you so passionate about this artifact?"

"Let's just say I have a personal interest in this cylinder..."

"What do you mean?"

"I've been having these dreams lately."

"Dreams?"

"Yes. About a harem tent. And a young new slave, learning the dance. Learning a new life. One far different from the future she was bred for....What is it, Mirza?"

He is staring at me with intense wonder.

"This is going to sound really strange...but as you said that, I just saw you in this tent you speak of, as the dancer...but also as you!" A kind of déjà vu."

My hands start to shake, "This woman...she was someone's beloved. But she's being held prisoner in this dream. In this camp. Far from the young man who loves her. And somehow they meet again. This girl and her beloved. THAT is my dream."

"And after I dreamed this, I translated the cuneiform on this cylinder...and the stories MATCH!"

Now he is stroking my hand. Drinking me in.

"And here we are again...lovers that were never meant to be," he finally said, after a long silence.

I pull my hand away as if scalded.

"Why did you *say* that? You're *scaring* me! That's exactly what the young man says in my dream."

He shrugs with pretend casualness, "It just popped into my head... Sorry. How about this: Did you know you have some powdered sugar on your nose..."

Tension broken, I slap at him playfully and giggle. Touch a finger to the top of one of the cookie and dust the tip of *his* nose with the powder. I've never been this forward with a man before.

The Secret of the Cylinder

Enough of dreams for now...I slip into the present and laugh; just enjoying the attentions of this exquisite man who is also clearly liking my company.

“” 8 “”

A Goddess by any other Name

Anoush sits at a carrel at the Tehran University library. She still wears her "uniform"—white oxford shirt and Levis, but breaking her own protocol, the top two buttons are undone. Her ponytail, usually pulled tightly back, is loose, with tendrils of hair framing her face. She is even wearing a brush of mascara and a light blush on her cheeks and lips.

A book lies before her, open to a yellowed page, that shows a figurine of the goddess Inanna. Inanna is naked and cupping her breasts with her hands, like an offering.

Mirza sneaks up behind her. Peers over her shoulder. His eyes widen.

"That's a lovely lady, Anoush. But she's a little...voluptuous for me."

Anoush snaps the book closed, reddening.

"You wouldn't know a goddess if you met one," she says, swatting at him playfully.

He jumps back. "But I'm standing right behind one..." He chuckles.

"And one who nearly wears her heart on her sleeve." His gaze rests on the heart-shaped birthmark Anoush bears just below her right collarbone.

"I don't mean *me*, silly." She blushes and adjusts her blouse to cover the heart. Shrugs. "And I've had this birthmark longer than I've had sleeves."

"OK, then, who is *that* goddess and why is she more important than *this* one?" Mirza's fingers graze her shoulder.

Anoush clears her throat. Reopens the tome to its bookmarked page.

"Inanna—Sumerian goddess of love, fertility and warfare. She took the heroine's journey into the underworld and returned, queen of strength and shadow."

"Well, we need to choose mentors this week for our thesis projects. I say give her a call..." Mirza deadpans. Anoush smiles and let out a good-natured, exasperated sigh.

He looks at his watch. "Is it *that* late? I have an exam first thing tomorrow... Would you like me to walk you home?"

"No, but thanks. I have more work to do here before I head out."

"All right then, m'lady..." With a kingly bow, Mirza walks away. Anoush shakes her head, smiles, and bends over her book again.

~

Hours later, as Anoush begins to nod off over her tome, her roommate Omid passes behind her. Her eyes widen when she sees the goddess image. She touches Anoush on the shoulder, making her jump.

"*Here* you are! You'll never have a life, not to mention a boyfriend, if you spend your nights in the library!"

A Goddess by any other Name

Sleepily, Anoush says, "Oh, hey, Omid. I'm working on my thesis project."

"*That?*" Omid points wide-eyed to the page with the statue.

"Not exactly...I've stumbled across something even more amazing! She's connected to it, but...look at this," Anoush pulls over another book of Sumerian text. "Here!" Her finger jabs at an indecipherable phrase.

"A clay cylinder. From 500 BC. Not like the ones you've seen commissioned by Cyrus or Nabonidus. This one tells the story not only of a woman, but a concubine! And a prince's beloved and betrothed! This is seriously counterculture."

Omid shrugs and rolls her eyes. Examines her long, red nails. Her interest in politics only goes so far as who gets in quickly at the local disco, and doesn't have to wait in line with the plebes behind the velvet cordon.

Anoush pulls over a third book, points to an image of the Cyrus Cylinder. "It would look like this...and if what I'm reading is still accurate, it's at the National Library."

Omid sighs. "Your research could get you into a lot of trouble. These are dangerous times, Noosh."

Anoush sighs, "Oh, don't be an old, worrying aunt!"

"I'm serious! Keep your head down!"

Anoush waves her away, "Good night, Aunty! I'll be fine. And I'll be home soon."

Omid walks away, shaking her head. Anoush resumes poring over her ancient texts.

A Goddess by any other Name

☙ ۹ ❧

Library

Anoush stood outside the imposing entrance to the National Library. The solid musculature of rearing white horses flanked either side of enormous wooden doors, which were thankfully still open to the public. Her heart fluttered as she climbed the marble stairs. Stepping into its mausoleum-like interior, she blinked as her eyes adjusted to the darkness. Dust motes swam before her eyes in the slices of sunlight that beamed in from clerestory windows.

She approached the heavy wooden information desk, where a hook-hosed, hollow-eyed man stood, sorting through a card catalog; making a show of pulling out an occasional card, and throwing it into a pile with a scowl or a triumphant flourish.

He didn't look up for several minutes. She cleared her throat. Training an inkjet eye on her, he furrowed his brow, as if she were interrupting the shah himself from his doomsday duties.

"May I help you?" he sighed.

"Mr. Zare," she read off his name tag. "I'm a history grad student at Tehran University. I'm working on my Master's thesis project about a couple of 'lost' artifacts from the time of Darius."

"And why is this important?"

The Secret of the Cylinder

She opened an ancient tome that she'd walked in with and pointed to the page that bore the cylinder. Taking a deep breath, she charged ahead:

"I have reason to believe, from this book, that this cylinder was commissioned by puppet-king Belshazaar II of the Babylonian satrapy in 497 BC. What sets it apart from any other cylinder of its kind, is that it contains the story of a woman! Not chronicles of temples or ziggurats spruced up for political reasons. Not tallies of grain or tithes sent to the king. No boasts about one's magnificence. Not even a story about his wife Vashti. I've been translating the Sumerian cuneiform, which, it seems, no one has bothered to do until now."

At this, the cleric held up a hand, which she ignored.

"This cylinder tells the story of a concubine, named Amat. Belshazaar's former fiancée and beloved.

"Young lady," he snapped. "There's no place in our history for whores! Why bother with such nonsense? Our new regime has plans for disposing of such garbage." He patted the stack of cards on his desk righteously.

"But, Mr. Zare, this cylinder, and the statue of Inanna which accompanied it, have a very important role in our past...and our future!"

He leaned over the counter threateningly.

She took a step back.

"No one is interested in that old heresy. You should just go home were you belong. And wear a chador! Show some respect!"

Library

Anoush eyed his stack of cards...history about to be erased. The history of women.

Noticing her stare, Zare continued, "In fact, it's my task to classify our abundance of such objects prior to their disposal...to make sure we track down, then erase all such abominations from our glorious history...and future!" He suddenly looked put-upon by the ponderous task.

Anoush brightened.

"Mr. Zare...I could help you with the archiving...if I could just first take a look in this bin." She pointed to the bin number in the Sumerian antiquities text she'd brought.

Zare held her with his penetrating gaze, like a bug at the end of a pin, then sighed, "I can't believe I'm doing this....Very well then. Come with me. You can finish your translation, so we can solve her mystery, and close her case. You have one hour!"

He led her to a back room, where on a forgotten shelf, among many crumbling containers, lay a dusty shoe box.

As he retreated, she put on the cotton gloves and a mask he'd given her. Holding her breath, she lifted the cover of the box.

The cylinder was not there.

The Inanna statue *was*, however; enclosed in a baggie, like a sandwich. A small slip of paper beside the statue said that the cylinder had been relocated to Qavam House at Eram Garden in Shiraz. A nine hour drive north.

She lifted the statue with trembling hands. *Nice archival storage.*

Scribbling furiously, she began describing the statue in her notebook...including how it had a heart-shaped carnelian set below the right collarbone. *What?!* Her hand flew absently to her own collarbone. *No time to think!* She copied the contents of the note about the cylinder, and then went on to Zare's stack of index cards; pulling out and neatly describing each item on a card. The list contained a treasure trove of artifacts from a more Goddess-friendly era.

Too soon, Zare reappeared, tapping his watch. "Time's up!"

"But I'm not finished!"

"Yes you are."

He eyed her open notebook and the goddess statue lying in the box. Snatching up her notebook, the box, and cards, he straightened and towered over her; only a tiny desk separating her from his menacing presence.

"Hey, that's mine!" she protested, reaching for her notebook, but then recoiling at the sight of the gnarled hand that was holding it. Several fingers were missing.

"Antiquities and their historical review by experts are the property of the government."

"Which government?"

"The new one, to which I belong," he pronounced. Grabbing her by the elbow, he tore her from the room. A chador-clad assistant appeared, and he handed her the box. A brief flash of interest passed over the woman's face as she gazed at the statue, before she steeled it into a blank wall. Her name tag read Mrs. Mossadegh.

"Destroy this thing!" he said to her. The woman reached out a scarred, reddened hand to take the statue from Zare. She glanced briefly at Anoush, expressionless.

The cleric grabbed the fuming student by the arm and escorted her to the library exit. He gave her a push out the door, causing her to stumble down the stairs and nearly wrench her ankle.

"Your work is done here, woman. And so is mine, with that thing. Don't come back, or I'll call the authorities."

He dusted off his hands and pushed the ponderous doors closed with a clatter and clunk.

Shaking with fury, Anoush stood, holding onto the railing for dear life.

"How dare you!" she hissed, impotently, to the closed door.

She spun on her heel and strode to her yellow VW Beetle, as the tears that had been at bay and smarting her eyes now clouded her vision.

When she reached the car, she suddenly glimpsed a vision in her minds eye of the cleric with a different face, bellowing from a throne in a tent. At her. She looked up at him from a prone position on the sand. Blood drummed in her ears as she trembled with anger and humiliation.

Anoush shook her head, twisted the car door handle and crumpled into the seat. She pounded the steering wheel. Rested her head against it. Then with a sigh, she opened the glove compartment, fished out a notebook and pen, and began writing furiously.

When she'd written all she remembered, she slumped in the seat and gazed back at the library. A scowling stranger now stood

outside its door, shifting his weight between his feet. The giant doors opened and the chador-clad woman exited. The man grabbed her hand and practically dragged her down the street.

Intrigued, Anoush started her car and followed them at a safe distance. They ducked into a mosque, and Anoush parked nearby. She fashioned a headscarf out of a kerchief that was lying on the passenger seat, and slipped into the mosque. Approaching the women's section, she casually knelt next to the librarian.

"Mrs. Mossadegh, I need your help," Anoush whispered.

The woman gasped, held a finger to her lips. "We do not speak here!" she whispered urgently.

"I need that figurine from the library. The one that Zare told you to destroy."

The woman shooks her head. "What makes you think I didn't dispose of it?" The librarian's eyes looked frightened and suspicious. She pulled up her sleeve to reveal her burnt hand. Anoush recoiled.

"How do you think I got this? From sticking my nose where it didn't belong."

"You don't have to live in fear. We don't need to live in fear. That statue is part of our past...and future, as women! And, believe it or not, there are men who care about this too."

"Shhhhh!" hissed some nearby women.

"I won't leave until you agree to meet with me...with the statue."

The librarian glanced about worriedly, then bent her head to Anoush's, "Meet me in Jamshidieh Park, The Garden of Ferdowsi

by the new Vaziri sculpture, tomorrow at 2 p.m... And my name is Lila."

~

The next day, Anoush walked to the appointed place, and sat on a bench by the rather Olmec-looking sculpture by Naser Houshmand Vaziri. Like a squat giant, the cement god sat in lotus position with his hands pressed to his cheeks, eyes wide open circles, belly exposed. He appeared to be as horrified by recent political events in Tehran as Anoush was.

About five minutes later, Lila approached, holding the hand of a skipping young girl. Chatting briskly with her daughter, the mother approached the bench upon which Anoush sat.

She turned to her daughter, "Go play close by, Atoosa."

As the five-year-old girl ran off, the mother sighed, and returned her gaze to Anoush.

"Your daughter is beautiful," Anoush beamed.

"Thank you...Listen." Suddenly serious, Lila leaned in toward Anoush. "There's something I need to know before we go any further."

Anoush blanched and took a deep breath.

"Yes?"

"Your name."

"Anoush," she giggled nervously.

"Why is this so important to you?", Lila asked, resting her hand on the cloth-wrapped a bundle she'd set down between them.

"Forgive me for being blunt, Lila, but freedoms your daughter doesn't even know she has are about to be taken away from her. I'll keep that statue safe. Promise. We need to remember. No one should have to live in fear."

Lila looked toward her laughing daughter, who was just returning with a sprig of jasmine in her hair. The gaze that met Anoush's was thoughtful.

"May you bring freedom back to our land," she smiled as she pushed the statue toward Anoush.

A feeling of profound peace stole over Anoush as she touched the bundle.

She knew she was doing the right thing.

❧ 10 ☙

Back at the Coffee House

"I see you have that tome with you again," Mirza smiles, as I settle across from him at "our" coffee house again.

"How have our dreams been?"

"The same," I reply, "and I've translated more of the cuneiform." I eagerly open my book.

"Look!" I point to the cuneiform, reading it, "She made the ultimate sacrifice for another harem sister. Even though she was head harem girl, she gave up her life; standing up for what she believed in...a life without oppression."

"I have to do this...I have to steal this cylinder, and hide it in a safe place. Before it's destroyed by the clerics."

Sadly he shakes his head, "but why?"

"Because we need a message of freedom here, now...of hope...to counteract what's happening."

"And...I already have the Inanna statue that seems to be the

companion piece to the cylinder."

"How did you get it?"

I tell him of my experience at the library and afterwards with Lila.

Mirza signs deeply as his soulful eyes search mine. "I see your mind is made up to follow this thing through...All right. Let me help you. Where *is* this cylinder?"

"According to the note I found at the National Library, it's at the mansion at Eram Garden in Shiraz: Qavam House."

He whistles. "The mansion is a museum for Pahlavi University. Do you think our student cards will gain us access there?"

"I think we have a chance."

"Then it's onto Shiraz! Let me make sure we can get in there. By the way, do you have a chador?"

"No, my family is liberal. "

"It would help get you in at Pahlavi without as many questions. These days..."

"I know."

"We can borrow one from my sister. I'll give it to you after class, Friday."

A million scenarios rush through my head, but above everything is the realization that he's willing to support what I believe in! A glowing warmth spreads through me from head to toe.

Back at the Coffee House

ೞ 11 ಐ

A Chador to cause some Chatter

Friday

I sit a couple desks behind Mirza, as the professor drones on. Oddly, there is a YSL shopping bag by his chair. Most of the girls are stealing surreptitious glances at it. A murmur of conversation causes the professor to sternly silence the young ladies. All I can see is a hint of black fabric within the mystery bag.

Is he trying to be funny? Hiding a chador in a couture bag?

Finally, class is over. Mirza scoops up his books and—with that grin that makes me melt—tilts his head toward the door.

In the hallway, he hands me the bag, "Your chador, mademoiselle. I will collect you from your apartment at 8 a.m. on the 30th."

He is being mysterious and I am totally confused.

"I thought we were going to Pahlavi as students on a research project."

The Secret of the Cylinder

"I came up with a better idea," he beams and shoos me and my questions away with his hand.

In the ladies room, I open the bag and unroll the distinctively un-chadorly silk. My jaw drops at the gorgeous cocktail dress I am holding. At the bottom of the bag is an invitation to a New Years' Eve party at Qavam House.

This man seems to have some magical powers.

❧ 12 ❧

The Hathor Ammon – The Hidden One

Shefar gazed across the desert at the approaching caravan with cold reptilian eyes. He scratched his chin, intrigued. Behind a dozen sentry, bearers held a palanquin aloft. Additional servants hovered a scarlet canopy over its occupant.

"Bring them to me!" He stabbed the air in the direction of the entourage and fixed a fierce eye on the bodyguard to his side.

"How do you wish us to handle them, sire?"

"As honored guests. But if you think they mean to deceive us, then kill them all."

"Yes, your grace."

~

Later, Shefar perched on his throne — a formidable figure in spite of his many physical issues. Hands that had fingers missing, and gnarled legs, however, could be overlooked if rich cloth covered them. The scar across his neck, from where his family had tried to

kill him was easily hidden as well, by a scarf.

Children with deformities were considered bad luck by his people. Left as a baby to die out in the night, it was only by the kind intervention of a local beggar woman that his life had been spared. Now, he owned a small but successful realm—a harem he'd stocked with rare and precious things. As king of his little fiefdom he reigned ruthlessly; feared by many, mocked by few.

As he faced his guests only his face was exposed, and this he steeled as much as he could into what, for him, was a smile. He beamed at his favorite concubine, Anath, who sat behind him. That brilliant, beautiful one, not young in years, but skillful and vibrant in heart, and the only one he cared about. She sat pensively, chin in hand, studying his fake grin, and shook her head almost imperceptibly, with a small grin of her own.

"My happy face is the same as my angry face, what can I say?" He muttered, and shrugged, returning his attention to the room before him.

Anath hid a giggle behind her hand.

The palanquined one was brought into Shefar's tent, along with six bodyguards. When the guest was set down, he lifted a billowy gold hood, and rose to a startling height. Shefar's guards gasped. The sheik himself nearly lost his composure. He could hear the zing of swords being unsheathed from their scabbards by his guards.

"Peace," Shefar barked to his men, with a wave of his hand. He turned to his guest.

The Hathor Ammon - The Hidden One

"I am Sheik Shefar. To what do I owe the pleasure of your acquaintance?" he boomed magnanimously.

The seven foot tall humanoid had a rather triangular head, almond-shaped eyes, and noticeably pointed ears. An Egyptian headdress covered its apparently bald crown. It was like nothing Shefar had ever seen before. Raising a huge, bony right hand with impossibly long fingers, the being said in a deep, resonant voice, "My name is Ammon...and we want what you want...Peace. And perhaps a trade."

"I'm intrigued," Shefar crooned craftily. "What do you offer for trade?"

The being nodded to one of his guards, and they brought over a cloth-covered item; whisking off the fabric to reveal a treasure box encrusted with priceless gems.

Shefar's eyes glinted with greed. He reached for the box. But the Hathor raised a hand again.

"There is more," Ammon said. "The inscription explains it: 'He who possesses this will be most powerful. Yet what most *think* is power will be taken by its touch.'"

"A riddle?" Shefar's mouth twitched. "But what does it mean?"

"There is only one way for you to find out," Ammon replied.

The Hathor Ammon – The Hidden One

Sensing deception, Shefar had one of his guards approach the box.

"You must actually reach in to experience the treasure," Ammon continued.

Shefar laughed and his men joined in, breaking the tension. Pushing out his chest, the guard strutted over to the box and lifted the lid. Light emanated from the container and the man hesitated again for a moment. Then with a shrug he reached in.

Half expecting the man to lose his hand or worse, Shefar was stunned when the man's features became peaceful, beatific, even. He straightened, closed the lid, and bowed to the Hathor. "Thank you, my Lord for sharing such a wonder with me."

"What, What, WHAT?" Shefar snapped. He stormed down from the dais, flipped open the box and repeated the guard's actions. His features jerked unnaturally into calmness, and the hand he lifted trembled.

Then a smirk broke the near-peaceful expression. "This is perfect. I can geld my enemy with such a thing as this!"

"Odd...with most, the effect lasts for a fortnight," said Ammon, thoughtfully.

"With most? Where are you from, exactly?" Shefar asked.

"Many a day's journey from here," Ammon replied cryptically.

The Hathor Ammon - The Hidden One

"I am not from here, and am also very different," boasted Shefar. "Not an ordinary human. But what of it? What would you like in exchange?"

"Your eldest concubine."

More laughter from the men. Shefar chuckled in disbelief. Was *this* a trick?

"Why the eldest, if I might ask," Shefar posed, glancing toward Anath, whose face was tight. She was helpless to help her mother—the eldest concubine—in this situation.

"We Hathors value wisdom above all. And wisdom is rarely in the youngest. It would be most precious to me to share minds with your wisest female."

Again Shefar's men giggled. Avoiding Anath's pleading gaze he bellowed, "Bring the one called Kiya."

Moments later, a distraught, elderly woman was dragged into the tent. She held Anath's gaze with wild eyes. When she looked upon the Hathor, however, she gasped and prostrated herself immediately. Her face beamed and her eyes glittered moistly when she rose, as if she were meeting the Creator himself.

"My good lady," Ammon said, "it is time for you to return to the bosom of your mother, Egypt."

Kiya pressed her fingers to her face, joyous tears running down her cheeks. "So it is all true. The stories of you that the elders told. The

statues..."

Ammon smiled and nodded.

"Thank you, my lord," she said to Shefar. "May I say goodbye to my family before I leave?"

"Do what you must," Shefar muttered, and waved her off, not comprehending the woman's reaction. He'd thought she'd be kicking and screaming.

"Who *are* you?" Shefar squinted.

"Just a traveler from a far land, come to do a little trading."

Shefar shrugged, accepted the box, and bade his men take care of the mysterious traveler and his entourage.

❧ 13 ☙

Should I stay or should I go?

Friday, later

Anoush sits at the edge of her bed. Staring at the YSL bag on the floor of her room, chin in hands.

Am I ready for this?

She stares at the goddess statue on the bed.

Is the world ready for this?

Her gaze returns to the YSL bag.

A slow smile spreads over her face.

"Omid!" she shouts, "Do you have a pair of black dress shoes I can borrow?"

Omid's face appears at the door. She chuckles and fetches the shoes.

Later, with Omid's work complete. Anoush gazes into her mirror, with makeup, updo, dangly earrings, heels, and THE DRESS. Wallflower no more; Anoush is a bombshell.

"Oh, and you might want these..." Omid slips her some condoms.

The Secret of the Cylinder

Anoush's face reddens, but she accepts them graciously.

Her other hand flies to her mouth, "What am I doing?"

"Destiny, dear. You've saved it up for long enough...Oh and also a service to your country, although they don't know it yet...not the sex, but the other thing."

A moment of silent tension.

They collapse against each other, laughing.

⌘ 14 ⌘

Flashback - Correcting the Cultic Mistake

"I carved my own heart out of carnelian and gave to my family my red, red love."
~ Normandi Ellis, from *Awakening Osiris,*
The Egyptian Book of the Dead

"As for me, Nabonidus, king of Babylon, save me from sinning against your great godhead and grant me as a present a life long of days, and as for Belshazzar, the eldest son -my offspring- instill reverence for your great godhead in his heart and may he not commit any cultic mistake, may he be sated with a life of plenitude." ~ Translation from the
Nabonidus Cylinder by Paul-Alain Beaulieu

The camp lay in ruin. All the sheik's henchmen lay dead. The women were gathered in a quietly joyful group. All but one. The one that mattered most to Belshazaar.

Panting raggedly from the carnage he and his men had created, he reentered the sheik's tent. Shefar lay where he'd left him, in a pool of blood.

The prince's eyes scanned the shadowy interior. A glint from

something behind the throne lured him to the dais. A box. Inlaid with jewels. It bore an inscription on its lid:

"He who possesses this will be most powerful. Yet what most *think* is power will be taken by its touch."

"I have nothing to lose!" Belshazaar muttered with a mirthless chuckle. His fingers tore open the lid.

"What the...!" He drew his hand away from the glowing contents, as if scalded. Then reached in. His finger left an impression on the moist surface of a box full of clay.

His breath evened out. His hands stilled. A peaceful expression stole over his features. He sank onto the sheik's sumptuous rug.

Blood on his hands began to disappear. Wounds closed.

As he stared with amazement at the box, one of his men called to him from outside. He snapped the lid shut. Rose. Tucking it under his arm, he strode out of the tent, not looking back.

As his caravan led the women away on camel and donkey, he turned back once to the ghostly tent village.

"With this gift, I will tell your story to the world, my Beloved," he whispered, patting the satchel in which the box lay. "You will live forever. The peace you now enjoy will be your legacy."

~

Flashback - Correcting the Cultic Mistake

A week later, Belshazaar leans over a serene scribe who shapes the clay into a cylinder. A statue in the shape of an ample-hipped woman offering her breasts lies on the scribe's table, nearly finished. A carnelian shaped like a little heart is inset just below her right collarbone. *Just like Amat's birthmark,* he mused. The workman's tools are arranged nearby, ready to incise the cuneiform characters onto the cylinder. He looks up expectantly, angelic smile on his face. The jeweled box is empty now.

"What would you have the cylinder say, sir?"

The prince clears his throat, "I was born of the desert, and to the desert I must return..." he begins.

Flashback - Correcting the Cultic Mistake

❧ 15 ❧

The Cylinder Speaks

Newly fashioned am I! What was formless now has shape, heft and voice! From Ammomati, Hunab Ku, Atum, the great void...to this. An instrument for humans to access their greatest potential.

The prince keeps me in the jeweled chest like a genie in a bottle, resting on a bed of opulent ivory silk. Every now and then when he is agitated he takes me out. Lies down with me resting on his chest like a cat. Only then does his grief lessen...for a little while.

~

But the genesis of my clay essence took place in the long ago...back on Sirius at the dawn of this Universe.

It is much later now. I try to remember all the hands that have held me throughout time after the Prince. All the faces that have gazed at me...some rapt, some greedy, some heartbroken. A blur of faces stretching through the ages.

Belshazzar died before his queen Vashti. After he departed, she sold me immediately to a traveling merchant. She'd always feared the connection between he and Amat—something I reminded her of. That kind of love scared her. Her marriage to Belshazaar was a political arrangement, not one of love, so she was eager to dispose of me as soon as she could.

The Secret of the Cylinder

After my quick dismissal from court, I bumped along in my box in the merchant's caravan for many days; the Inanna statue my close companion in what had become my tomb—what was once my womb, back when I was formless presence and pure potential.

A beautiful Egyptian priestess—Ita was her name—once held me aloft reverently in one hand, the Inanna statue in the other, in ceremony before an altar. We shimmered together for several years, until she met an untimely end; murdered by a greedy thief who spirited me away once again.

The jeweled box once glittered beneath the throne of a king who uses me to weaken his enemies.

Another time it sparkled beneath the bed of lovers who enjoyed my profound peace. That was a lovely time, where my purpose— though confined to influence just these two—was honored and valued for its true nature.

For a time I lay in a darkened bank vault, kept as a mere status symbol of wealth by a billionaire Japanese businessman. When his fortune fell, I was sold at an auction, where, miraculously, the statue and I were recognized as a true National Treasure, returned to Iran, and installed at Eram Baugh mansion.

Many lives. Many owners. So very many stories...

❧ 16 ☙

Making Yasmeen

12/30/1978

Mirza's shoulders finally relaxed, as they sped past Tehran's city limits.

"I wish airport security wasn't so ridiculous these days...flying would be so much quicker."

Anoush smiled and shook her head ruefully, "The country's upside down. I'm sure you made the right choice."

"Yeah, but nine hours?"

She turned to the road ahead and her hopeful expression vanished, "Oh my God, Mirza! What's that?"

"A checkpoint...but it's OK. It looks like the Shah's army."

"How can that be OK?"

"Just be cool. We're going to a New Years' Party at Qavam House, remember? That's all. We're innocent students that need to blow off some steam, and one of our professors gave us

tickets...Oh...shit!"

They watched in horror as the car before them was swarmed by armed soldiers. After a brief exchange, one ripped open the driver's door and hauled the man out. He pushed him roughly, face-first against the cab as another handcuffed him. The man struggled. One of the soldiers raised his AKM and hit the driver in the head with the butt end. The driver's knees buckled and they dragged him away. One of the soldiers drove the car off the road.

Then they waved Mirza forward.

"Shit. Shit. Shit..."

"Mirza!?"

"OK, just be cool," he repeated tightly, clearing his throat.

As their car rolled to a stop, the same two heavily armed soldiers approached each window, with a third training a rifle at Mirza.

Flashing his winning smile, and keeping his hands on the wheel, Mirza nodded to the guard then motioned with his head to the hangtag on his rear view mirror. The soldier at Mirza's side glanced at the tag, then nodded.

"Identification and nature of your trip, son?"

"Thank you, sir. Here you go...My godfather, Gholam Azhari, secured this travel pass. We're off to a New Years' Eve party at

Making Yasmeen

Qavam House at Eram Garden in Shiraz."

The soldier's eyes widened at the name. He gazed at the two, scrutinized their IDs and the hangtag.

Anoush attempted a weak smile and batted her eyelashes for the first time in her life.

To their amazement, the guard nodded again, and motioned for the other to lower his gun.

He waved them on. "Be careful out there..."

Shaking his head, he straightened and faced the other guard, "Crazy kids going to parties when the country's falling apart..."

"Sounds like the perfect thing to do when the world's coming to an end...sir," the other shrugged, as he scratched his thigh absently with his uzi.

~

Mirza stepped on the gas, as gently as he could, even though every cell in his body screamed at him to floor it.

Anoush released white knuckles from her handbag and sank into the seat.

"Mirza, you told me to just bring my drivers license and student ID. What exactly are these travel documents...and that hangtag?"

"A carte blanche anywhere in Iran as long as we stick to the main roads."

"Meaning?"

"I have an uncle who runs SAVAK, the Shah's National Security and Intelligence Organization. He's done some things. Knows some things...things that are proving helpful to his godson," he winked.

Mirza then explained exactly how *she* would steal the cylinder at Eram Garden.

"So these tools are..."

"In a bag in the trunk."

"Wow." She sighed heavily, gazing at the ribbon of road unspooling before them.

"I'm nervous, Mirza...What if we get caught?"

"We'll rehearse the plan a bunch of times before the party. And I'll be waiting right outside. When I leave you to schmooze with Professor Abbas by yourself, excuse yourself after a bit to go to the ladies room. Go to the one on the second floor. I'll leave the tools in the tank of the second stall... Thank goodness bell bottoms are still in style! I'll just have to be careful when I walk with the equipment strapped to my leg."

Making Yasmeen

~

Finally, they arrived at their hotel.

"Ah yes, Mr. and Mrs. Azhari..."

The clerk scrutinized Mirza over his spectacles. Anoush blushed furiously, but it went unnoticed.

"Let me upgrade you to the honeymoon suite."

Mirza and Anoush exchanged surprised glances.

"Sure...um, thanks!" Mirza shrugged.

"We want the Shah's favorites to be well cared for," the clerk replied. "Majid Moradi at your service," he bowed slightly.

After the bellboy had delivered their bags and the door closed behind him, they both leaned against it, shook their heads and laughed.

"I didn't realize you were such a celebrity."

"Celebrity is very tenuous these days..." Mirza sighed.

Anoush stared at the carpet. She was exhausted, exhilarated, and nervous. Of *course* she had to save the cylinder, but who were *they*? Kids, practically. Idealistic kids, but kids, nonetheless...She felt like

a criminal already, having seen so many guns pointed their way at the half dozen checkpoints they'd had to endure.

Mirza glanced at the worry now creasing her brow. He made a tcchh sound, and smoothed it away with his index finger, then kissed it.

She looked up at him solemnly, "It probably won't go away until we leave Shiraz...but anyway...thank you *so* much, Mirza, for all you've done...I hope you know your support means everything to me."

"I know," Mirza said with a broad smile.

He cupped her face with his hand and kissed her deeply. Her lips and body responded, fear momentarily forgotten.

He caressed her hair, "You are so lovely...my jasmine blossom..."

Holding her at arms' length for a second, he drank her in. Then drew her into another long kiss, until she was surrendering, happily, willingly....

"Wait!" she said breathlessly, breaking away with a smile. We've been driving for nine hours! I *really* need a shower."

"Absolutely, m'lady...I'll go find us some wine, and other comforts."

Fifteen minutes later, when she emerged, candles were burning,

chilled champagne awaited, and soft music wafted from a tape player on the dresser.

"Here! Sip, savor, and relax," he said as he handed her a flute of bubbly. "My turn."

When he appeared, all dimples and clean manflesh wrapped in white terry cloth like a present, she was blissfully reclining on the bed. She opened her eyes and admired the beautiful man who took a single red rose from a bud vase on the table, and presented it to her gallantly, with a bow.

"I...um...need to tell you something," she gulped, suddenly shy. "I... I'm a...."

"I know, love," he said with his dreamy smile. "Just let me adore you."

He undid her belt and teased the robe from her shoulders with little kisses, then unwrapped her completely.

"Mmmmm...absolute perfection," he sighed as he drank her in for a moment, then swooped in for a kiss.

~

He lavished her body with such tenderness that she opened to him like a flower. Burying his face in her mystery, he teased up passion that she'd never felt before. Her back arched as she convulsed with a sweet release, and only when he'd brought her to that place several times did he enter her ever so gently that she shuddered

and gasped again.

So this is what all the fuss is about, a part of her mind thought giddily.

Much later, they dozed in each others' arms, her silky hair strewn across his chest, her head resting in the hollow of his arm. Safe for now.

~

Late the next morning, New Years' Eve, they woke to make love again, bodies fitting perfectly, like they were made for each other.

By noon, they were able to discuss less romantic plans over room service, as they pored over Mirza's map of Qavam House. He indicated an upstairs room.

"Here's where it should be. You'll have to be very silent, love. Are you still sure you want to do this?"

"Absolutely," she pronounced as she stroked his thick, glossy hair. "After last night, I feel like I can do anything."

He pulled her to him hungrily.

~

"OK, now we need to get serious," he sighed, much later. He rose reluctantly and opened the small, mysterious black bag. "Let me

show you how the glass cutter works."

For the next several hours, they reviewed exactly what she should do, and where to exit and find him afterwards.

"You haven't breathed a word of our plan to anyone, have you?" he asked, searching her face. She looked away.

"Who?"

"Omid pretty much figured it out from my thesis work, and your invitation to Shiraz...She taught me all her hair and makeup tricks so I'd fit in at the party... Don't worry, my roommate wouldn't tell a soul."

"Are you sure?"

"Absolutely." She tried to quiet the little worm of doubt wiggling in the back of her mind. *I hope.*

They took a long walk to calm their nerves, napped, made love one more time, and at last, dressed in their finery and set off to the party.

~

Anoush's heels clicked on the paving stones as they approached the palace. Her head tipped back in wonder at the brilliantly lit edifice, fronted by its magnificent Persian Paradise garden. The mirrored porch swam with reflections from the pool, making her slightly dizzy. The night was cooling and the scent of jasmine

enveloped her as she took Mirza's hand and they made their entrance.

The grandeur inside stole her nerve. An incredible brilliance from three enormous chandeliers sparkled in a rainbow of colors off glass tiles set into the ceiling and walls.

Who do we think they are? We're in over their heads!

Mirza sensed her stiffen and pressed a reassuring hand to the small of her back. She took a deep breath, eyed him thankfully, and strode into the clinking, dazzling, chattering crowd.

A pleasantly tipsy Professor Abbas accosted them and introduced them to his associate, a Mr. Sorouch Zare, Department of Antiquities. His intense dark eyes gleamed with a reptilian coldness. Anoush was gripped with terror. *The librarian! Would he recognize her? All their careful planning could be for nothing. This could all end so badly in a heartbeat!*

"Dr. Zare, this is one of my stellar pupils, Banafsheh Bukhari," Professor Abbas boomed magnanimously, as he swept his arm in a grand gesture, taking in Anoush, and spilling some champagne on her in the process.

For a second, she saw Dr. Zare's features grow disfigured, menacing. Her spine tingled and she felt the urge to run away fast. She gasped, shook her head, and his features returned to the man before her who was now scrutinizing her with an amused glint in his eye.

"I often have that effect on women," he quipped drily. Dr. Abbas hooted.

Recovering, Anoush composed her face into the semblance of an innocent, starstruck student as she shook Sorouch's hand firmly.

"Please excuse me, I was just startled by the champagne baptism... Mr. Zare, I am *so* honored to be here in such an exquisite landmark, at the invitation of Professor Abbas," she gushed, hoping someone was believing her act. "You must visit palaces all the time..."

"Ah, yes, the enthusiasm of a novice," Mr. Zare responded witheringly. His eyes wandered, bored, across the room.

"And this is my other, stellar pupil, Vishpar Safavi...although his attention lately seems to be focused on things other than his studies..." professor Abbas chuckled.

Mirza reddened, but quickly reached for Mr. Zare's hand, with a smile.

"Let us hope these attentions don't cause anyone trouble," he said solemnly, looking into Mirza's eyes.

Mirza and Anoush glanced at each other quickly.

"Of course our students are modern and take precautions these days...." Professor Abbas interjected, still jolly and unflappable. "Education is a priority for our next generation. Children will come later, at the appropriate time."

"Of course," Mirza and Anoush chimed in unison, as they struggled with their smiles.

"That *is* what you meant, isn't it?" Abbas continued to Zare, raising an eyebrow, and appearing slightly concerned.

"Of course," Zare smirked. "Precaution...caution...is always advisable... I must go now. It was enlightening, meeting our most shining hopes for the future." The smile that never made it to his eyes left his lips immediately, as he turned on his heel and strode into the crowd.

Both Mirza and Anoush exhaled audibly.

"Don't worry, you two," Abbas consoled his rattled students, "he's always grumpy. Think nothing of it...It's the government issue underwear he's sporting. It's a bit too binding in some already tight places," he chucked. "And the way you both blushed at the same time...priceless! You're the picture of young, innocent love."

"Thank you *so* much for covering for us," Anoush gushed gratefully

"Yes, and thank you for a very informative introduction to Mr. Zare, Professor," said Mirza. "And we *will* be careful...please excuse me while I introduce Anoush to someone she needs to meet..."

For a second Mirza and Abbas' eyes met. Mirza realized then that the professor was completely sober, for all he'd been carrying on as

the University's drunk. Abbas raised a private toast to Mirza and they nodded in understanding.

Anoush pulled Mirza into a corner.

"Oh my God, Mirza...what if Zare's onto us!" In spite of Abbas' help, I felt like he could read our thoughts..."

"We don't know for sure, Noosh. So let's stick with the plan and pretend we're as innocent as Professor Abbas says we look, OK? You heard him . . . Don't worry . . . Zare knows nothing," Mirza declared a bit more bravely than he felt.

"Also, Abbas is just acting drunk. He's on our side."

"Oh thank God! Remember, I told you Zare was the cleric at the National Library who kicked me out after I researched the cylinder there."

"Yes, and it was all I could do not to punch him...Do you think he recognized you?"

"He didn't act like he did...And thanks to Omid's makeover, and new updo she taught me, I don't think I look at all like the geeky student he met the other day."

"We'll have to just carry on, as if he doesn't know you, then. And, um...sorry I 'forgot' about 'precautions' last night and this morning."

"Practice makes perfect," Anoush declared with a private smile. She kissed him.

The next hour or so passed with chitchat and barely tasted champagne as they mingled with the intelligentsia of the old and new guard, in a ballroom filled with incongruities, lies, and last hurrahs.

And then it was time.

One minute Mirza was leaning casually against a wall, surveying the crowd. The next, he was gone.

Anoush approached Professor Abbas again. He appeared just as tipsy and cheerful as before, and chatted eagerly with her. After a bit, she excused herself. As she turned to go, she felt him slip something into her hand, and give it a squeeze. She didn't look back at him.

~

Following Mirza's plans that they'd pored over studiously, Anoush raced lightly through the darkened upstairs halls, the disco music growing fainter below.

She retrieved the glass cutter from the upstairs lavatory and had just exited the ladies room when she had to press herself into a shadowy alcove as a guard shuffled by. She exhaled when he finally passed. Padded silently down another hallway. And then she was at her destination.

Making Yasmeen

There it was, in one of several display cases in the corner of a large room. Glowing slightly.

She felt a *frisson* slide up her spine and blood rush to her face.

It's now or never...

Peering right and left down the hall, she stepped into the room, and raced softly to the display case. Her heart filled as she looked down at the cylinder at last...her grail! All this study and longing. She felt almost blasphemous for what she was about to do, but she knew it was for the best.

Steeling her nerves, she set down the toolbag and pulled out the glass cutter. Looking around again surreptitiously, she set to her task. Freeing the cylinder.

Outside, in a back alley, Mirza rolled a Vespa into a shadowed spot. Then helplessly waited for the woman he loved.

Hurry, Noosh!

He gazed at his watch. Began pacing. Then stopped. *Oh shit! Don't want to call attention to myself.* He willed his mind peaceful and thought about the curves and delights he'd discovered in his treasure, only last night.

His heart began to radiate love, and suddenly he caught himself smiling, then worrying that this inner brilliance of his might single him out like a beacon, shining so brightly, as it was.

Making Yasmeen

~

An alarm sounded. Anoush burst outside. He gunned the Vespa and pulled up to the building. As he pulled her onto the seat behind him, he glimpsed a flash of someone on the street behind her. A woman? Just watching them. *Please keep us safe*, he prayed, as he willed her not to raise a gun or scream, whoever she was.

He tore into the alley; Anoush clutching him tightly. And then... a deafening roar. He found himself looking at the ground, as it approached him in slow motion.

How strange...

His last image was of Anoush falling away from him like a rag doll.

Noooo!!!

Intense pain.

A stab of searing sorrow.

And then...

Nothing.

❧ 17 ☙

A New Year

The room is stark—a cell practically—but the nurses are kind and generous with the morphine. Dingy gray walls, small windows...everything reflects my inner state.

How many days have I been here? I have no idea. It hurts to lift my head. I can't feel the left side of my face. I go from being fairly lucid and in excruciating pain, to a floaty haze.

Faces come and go. All strangers. Often a military uniform or a cleric, asking questions, questions, questions.

I know nothing. Not even my name. A girl with a pretty, round face stopped by today and said we were roommates. She gave me my name. Anoush. Even *this* tastes strange in my mouth. She said I was in an accident. I tell her the questions the men ask, and she says it's a blessing I know nothing right now.

Did I really commit treason and steal a national treasure? And who was the man they found me with? Omid says just a friend.

Bit by bit, memories return. And I become more and more scared. One day my bandages are removed and I get to see my new face.

The horror that is my new life gets worse and worse. Omid cannot

help me the day I am pronounced fit enough to be taken to a prison.

Why didn't they just let me die? The searing grief that consumes me daily over losing Mirza alternates with a numbness and hopelessness. They told me he died in the explosion.

I hear tidbits of what's going on outside the barbed wire from the other women; some of whom have visitors. The Revolution is underway...

Omid visits regularly, filling me in too. My family has all "disappeared" as well as Mirza's godfather and Professor Abbas. The world I'd known has changed utterly.

One day when I feel I can take it no longer, however, Omid gives me a ray of hope. She whispers to me about her role in rescuing the cylinder. She said she knew it was what I would have wanted, back when she made that split-second decision in the alley behind Qavam House. She knew I'd be taken to a hospital. The information I might have would be too valuable to the clerics for them to let me die. And without any evidence, no one could pin the theft on either Mirza or myself. Not right away, anyway. He and I were just students on a scooter.

Mr. Sorouch Zare visits me several times before my memory returns. And then afterwards, where I play the most convincing acting role of my life, pretending I still know nothing.

Omid flies off to Paris where relatives live and takes the cylinder with her. They put it in a safety deposit box.

A New Year

And I am left in my box of despair.

Miraculously, I am released from prison. They have given up on me and figure I am useless in their case. I will never be safe again in my country. I am being watched.

Omid smuggles me out of the country, using the fake passport and the new identity Professor Abbas had pressed into my hand at the New Year's Eve party. Omid kept that secret safe until it was needed as well.

We get out just in time. The shah is overthrown shortly afterwards.

A New Year

☙ 18 ❧

Written in the Stars

Montmartre, Paris, March, 1979

Anoush stared at the bread on the tray before her. It seemed to mock her. How dare it offer her life and sustenance when her beloved was dead. A few crumbs had fallen off onto the plate and she poked them absently, feeling their crusty texture, caraway seeds sticking to her finger. She pinched a seed between her fingernails and inhaled its sharp, spicy aroma. It didn't make her any more interested in the bread. Her mouth was as dry as this crust. She didn't care. She had stopped feeling hunger days ago.

The chicken soup whose smell made her nauseous had long gone cold on a nearby table. Anything she ate came up anyway, so why bother? With a sigh, she realized she'd need to get up soon and flush the soup down the toilet, so nobody would take her to task for not forcing down a meal she did not want. She'd promised her best friend that she'd eat something. Just as she'd lied the day before. And the day before that. A dullness had settled in her mind, so that it was a motionless, gray sea. A foggy corridor of nothingness. Everyone had hopes the move would lift her spirits, but it seemed nothing would.

Her limbs were leaden, emaciated. Her face — a stiff, painful mask on one side, where the blast had seared her skin. Her only physical reminder of their final moments together. That and one tiny photo propped by her bedside, next to the cold soup. Dimpled chin, Elvis hairstyle…such a handsome, carefree face. She'd led him to his

death, and what did she have to show for it of any value or meaning? She gazed down at the thin, throbbing vein on her wrist with fascination. They only allowed her plastic utensils.

How could it all have gone so wrong? She kept reliving the details in her mind. One moment, she was an idealistic student, in love for the first time…Stealing a national treasure, so it could be saved for future generations that would recognize its value. She and Mirza were gallant heroes, where below, out on the street, he waited with his Vespa, while she extracted the artifact from its glass prison on the upper floor of Qavam House. In Shiraz. On New Years Eve. Seemingly a thousand miles away. A thousand years ago. She'd tripped an alarm on her way out, but had eluded the guards, burst out the agreed-upon back door, climbed on the thrumming scooter, and they'd fled down the dark alley.

Then the deafening boom, darkness and silence…

It was only when she woke in a hospital bed that Omid filled her in on what had happened….and where the cylinder resided. Omid had been standing by the exit door of the mansion when Anoush raced out. How can roommates and best friends keep secrets? They can't, and Omid had followed Anoush and Mirza on their last night together, wary of Anoush's hairbrained scheme.

She watched helplessly as the Vespa veered off, and then disappeared in a thunderous cloud of smoke. Omid had raced over and from Anoush's lifeless hand, grabbed her purse, which contained the cylinder, some folded paper, a fake passport from professor Abbas, and a hotel key. Against her better judgment, she ran away as heavy footsteps approached.

Omid then proceeded to Anoush's hotel and, since Anoush had called Omid and told her their room number and combination to the hotel safe, should anything go wrong, Omid was able to

quickly extract the figurine and slip out before hotel security was onto anything.

It was only much later that Omid was able to return the cylinder to Anoush, after Omid smuggled them to Paris, to an anonymous apartment on Rue Ravignan, where they were safe. Where even Anoush's parents would not have been able to find her…if they'd been spared from the Ayatolla's wrath in the aftermath of the cylinder's theft.

~

Safe at last, in Paris, thanks to her best friend's bravery, Anoush pulled a velvet pouch out from under her pillow. She eased the cylinder out of its bubble wrap and sheath and held it cupped in her palms. Its surface was covered with little bird-like scratchings and starlike symbols. A story in cuneiform. She began tracing a line of text, whispering, "I was born of the desert and to the desert I must return. By the time you read this, my bones will be ground into dust and scattered to the four winds, like the shifting, searing sands…"

Oddly, the clay suddenly darkened in one spot. Then in another. She realized her tears were falling on it and marveled that she could cry anymore. It was as if just her face were crying. Her heart was still a heavy stone.

She wondered if this was how she would die, among crumbs and a cuneiform cylinder that bore the story of an ill-fated princess. The breadcrumbs before her couldn't lead her back to her own princess moments…the times she'd spent with Mirza in this life.

A searing pain tore through her head. With the shock of recognition, she saw images of the days back in Basra when he was her betrothed and even before that, her childhood friend. Racing through her parents' hallways as a young girl, and then again in

her wedding robe, dancing and holding aloft the red carnelian on her ring finger.

Another pain struck like a lightning bold, and she was back at Tehran University, sitting behind Mirza. She couldn't help but smile. He was so handsome and funny! He'd embarked on a series of happy ambushes; distracting her from her homework in the library. And then they went to a coffee house together. And fell in love. She'd been so shy! But so intrigued!

He'd actually been interested in her research about the cylinder, when it had been created by Prince Belshazaar in 500 BC—a heartbroken gesture to honor his beloved Amat, after he'd arrived too late to rescue her from the Sheik's camp.

Belshazaar's previous betrayal of Amat had haunted him; he'd let his family persuade him to disavow her, after her father had betrayed Belshazaar's father, the king.

Her family had been executed, and she'd been kidnapped and sold into a new life as a harem slave. And so, in a full circle of creation to destruction to creation, Belshazaar immortalized her on the cylinder…

This cylinder that kept darkening with more salty drops.

And then she was in the hotel room in Shiraz. Where she, Anoush, and Mirza had made love…for the first time…the night before the cylinder heist. That hotel room, where they'd plotted how to leave the New Year's party at the appropriate time and steal the precious object from its display case.

~

Written in the Stars

Anoush traced her fingers over the characters and a shiver ran up her spine. A small electrical jolt passed between the clay and her flesh. And just then she felt a sudden pinch in her womb. As she placed a cold, frail hand against her abdomen, an idea began to form like a tiny ghost in her clouded mind. The corners of her mouth twitched slightly. A deep peace stole over her.

~

When Omid entered the room moments later, Anoush was munching the bread. With bright, moist eyes, Anoush leveled her glance at her best friend's.

 "Well look at you…Welcome back to the land of the living! This is the first time I've seen you smile in months."

 "Hey, O…I need a favor. I think I heard of a place on Rue des Abbesses where I could get a…test."

"A test?" Omid gazed at Anoush searchingly for a moment, then noticed the hand over belly. She smiled. "Am I going to be a godmother?"

Anoush patted the cylinder, whose history lay between them, and bound her to her unborn child. She nodded. "I think it's written in the stars."

She reached out to her friend. Omid came over and received her second surprise of the day, as Anoush pulled her into a very life-affirming kiss.

Written in the Stars

19

Harem Girl

Omid left Anoush's room in their Paris apartment with a smile on her face. The smile faded when she passed a mirror in the hallway. The face that looked back from the glass was not the round-faced Omid, but that of a thin, hollow-eyed 18-year-old wearing a Scythian headdress. A six-inch tall cylindrical cap of gold brocade rested on her head, draped with red silk. On either side of her face, gold squares embellished the rich, ruby fabric in a stripe down both selvedges. Trails of glass beads fringed the lower edge of the gold cap. She was an exquisite prize.

As she gazed at the teardrop-shaped beads, she fell into the mirror...

~

She had been thrown onto a sandy floor that was covered with an ornate rug. Hot tears stung her eyes and her head pounded. She spun around just in time to see Amat's standing body slump, the sheik's dagger embedded to the hilt in her chest. As her savior's lifeless form fell to the ground, the sheik took a step back.

"Enough!" a woman's voice shouted, and both Shefar and the harem girl turned to see Anath, his favorite courtesan, striding boldly up to the sheik.

"I meant to punish the new one," Shefar said, almost petulantly.

"If you kill off all your girls, you won't have much of a harem, now will you?" Anath continued, struggling to calm herself and mollify the sheik.

To the harem girl's amazement, he nodded and simply watched as Anath led the pregnant newcomer off to safely.

~

Back in the women's tent, Anath held the girl close as she sobbed.

"Amat was also with child, dear. The child of a prince. A child that had no future, just like her mother. She has given you and your baby your lives in exchange for hers. Be worthy of her sacrifice, yes?"

The girl nodded, shaking.

~

This skill Omid had of appearing differently depending on her focus served her well, when she had showed up as an old lady to visit Anoush in prison. The guards and even Soroush never took her to be anything other than a compassionate and nosy, if harmless crone.

It didn't serve her well when she stepped out of the house in Paris, later that day, however, when suddenly she noticed she was being

watched. She'd been Omid, thinking herself Omid, as she left the house. Soroush Zare recognized her immediately from across Rue Ravignan and lifted a gun. Before he could fire, however Omid had fired her Beretta 950 that she always kept with her, flattening him instantly. Another shot rang out and Omid fell to the pavement. Just as Zare's lackey turned to run, a gendarme had stepped onto the street.

"Arretez! ARRETEZ! BOOM!

Zare's lackey fell dead.

Anoush watched all of this unfold from her bedroom window. As she crumpled away from the glass, she saw in its pearlescent opacity, herself as Amat, pushing the harem girl to safety, and taking the sheik's dagger. An ancient debt had been paid forward. This time around, she got to keep both her life and that of her baby's. So much bloodshed. So many lost. Now the disco queen, who'd used fashion and frivolity as a cover. With every muscle aching, Anoush tore herself up and out of the bed, and made it down the stairs, just as the medic arrived.

As she burst out of the house, she glanced to where Zare and his lackey had been lying. Zare was gone; a trail of blood leading off into an alley. Then her attention was drawn to a more pressing matter.

"Elle vit. Elle vit!" the medic confirmed to the police, and hearing this, Anoush fell to her knees, inwardly praising Inanna and all the helping spirits that were watching over her friend.

~

Harem Girl

Under a crisp and clear fall sky, Anoush pushed a stroller beneath a canopy of red-leafed oaks that fringed the rolling grounds of the rehab hospital. She entered the flower and balloon-festooned room where Omid lay in bed.

"There she *is!*" Omid gushed, as Anoush picked up baby Yasmeen and delivered her to the eager arms of her godmother. Omid covered the baby's face with kisses, as Anoush bent to kiss her best friend.

"How are you doing, O?"

"Much better. I can walk by myself now. They say I'll be released within a week or so."

"I am *so* happy for you! And for me. I'm going to need a babysitter soon," Anoush chuckled. "Oh, by the way, I brought you something else."

She placed a small shopping bag on the bed next to Omid and began pulling out nail polish, hair spray, and a pair of high heels.

"It'll be a long time before I can manage those," Omid sighed, gazing at the shoes. "I just started walking again, remember?"

"Well, then, the two of you will just have to learn how to walk like ladies together," Anoush joked, as she slipped the oversized shoe onto Yasmeen's tiny foot.

❧ 20 ☙

Reciprocity from a Harem Girl

An 18-year-old Anoush scans a bulletin board in the lounge of a dorm, clutching her schoolbooks to her chest. She tears off a slip of paper bearing a phone number from a fringe at the bottom of a sheet advertising "Roommate Wanted". Across the room, a dark-haired girl watches her with a smile on her face, as she leans against a wall.

Feeling eyes on her, Anoush turns quickly, sees the observer and suddenly feels dizzy. As she tumbles to the floor, she sees before her, not a fellow student, but a young woman with a Scythian headdress, falling away from her, as if she's been pushed. Just as she notices her own hands held out in the direction of the other girl, palms facing the stranger, she feels a stabbing pain in her chest and blacks out.

When Anoush awakens on the floor of the dorm's lounge, the dark-haired moon-faced girl is hovering over her. Concerned students are pressed close, then helping her up. Anoush shakes her head, feeling embarrassed. "What happened?" she says.

"You were tearing off a slip from my roommate ad and then you blacked out," says Omid. "Well, you certainly have my attention now! Let me tell you about the apartment..."

The Secret of the Cylinder

ೞ 21 ೞ

Flesh of this Earth

"This just in on CNN... The Cylinder of Amat has just been reported missing en route from Palestine to Pakistan. The world is stunned that this instrument of world peace has suddenly disappeared, just when its effects on Pakistan were once again wearing off.

This incident could upset the strategic balance the United Nations has worked out by moving the Cylinder of Amat, or COA to the next country most in need of it; weekly, sometimes daily."

Yasmeen stood transfixed before her television screen.

"The statue!" Tahj squealed.

"Not now Tahj," Yasmeen waved toward him.

The phone rang.

"Yes, we are shocked and horrified." She covers the mouthpiece, "Tahj, go see grandma. (Tahj runs into the other room). "Let me see if she's up to making a statement." "Mom?"

A moment later Anoush appears, led by Tahj. She is smiling. "Tell

them I'll make a statement," she says.

~

In a scrubby desert, a modern caravan crosses the border of Pakistan from India. From a military jeep, one of many, an aloof turbaned Pakistani man steps out to meet them. Tension. An Indian man steps out of the first of his contingent of jeeps. He offers something wrapped in a cloth to the Pakistani, who hesitates briefly, frowns, then shrugs and accepts it. As soon as he touches the gift, the Pakistani man breaks into a joyous smile. He opens the cloth. It's the Inanna statue, made from the same clay as the Cylinder of Amat. Raising it to the heavens, he opens his arms wide and give a brotherly hug to the Indian man.

The men rock silently together in an unlikely embrace, as phone cameras capture the moment of yet another miracle. A miracle carried through to the future from 500 BC and the love between two star-crossed souls, whose hearts were nonetheless as strong as the imperishable stars.

"Until we meet again, my Beloved," Anoush whispered as she gazed at the image on her TV of the two former enemies hugging and the statue held aloft in triumph; its carnelian sparkling in the sunlight for a heartbeat.

✿ 22 ✿

What was Lost is Found

The phone rang. "I'll get it!" Tahj piped as he raced across the living room.

"Grandma, it's for you. Some man." He shrugged and held the phone out.

Anoush strode over and held the receiver to her ear. She blanched and quickly felt for a chair. "How is that possible? Yes! Yes, I do. Tell me where..."

"What is it, Mom?" Yasmeen asked warily, noticing her mother's discomfort.

"Quick, get me a pen and paper," instructed Anoush. She hastily scrawled down several lines and then put down the phone, turning slowly to Yasmeen.

"Your father is alive and would like to see us."

"WHAT?"

"HOW?" Yasmeen blurted.

"Grandpa's...alive?" Tahj wondered, eyes wide.

The Secret of the Cylinder

"He said it's a long story. One he wants to tell us in person. He's in town, and wants to meet us at a special place in the Louvre tomorrow morning."

"Yippee!" Tahj squealed and began jumping up and down.

"Grandpa's back!"

Anoush stared at Yasmeen, dumbfounded.

After all this time.

I don't even know what to feel first.

She took a deep breath, picked up a vase and hurled it across the room. The pottery shattered spectacularly, causing Tahj to stop jumping and cringe.

"What's wrong, Mommy? Why isn't Grandma happy?"

Yasmeen gingerly approached her now sagging mother. She placed a tentative hand on Anoush's shoulder, then, seeing that no additional ceramics were about to become airborne, pulled her into her arms and hugged her fiercely.

After a moment she then turned to Tahj. "Grandma's been alone for a very long time. She's upset that Grandpa was taken away from her. It's hard for her to adjust to a big change like this, sweetie."

"But he's back now," he whined softly.

"It'll be OK," Yasmeen whispered to the trembling woman in her arms.

"Come here, Tahji. It'll be OK."

What was Lost is Found

~

Anoush fussed as the taxi pulled up before the Louvre. The dread she felt mixed strangely with a guarded, girlish joy.

If he'd survived the accident, why hadn't she heard from him until now? Why had he stayed away, all those years while she raised Yasmeen without him? With Omid's help, of course, but no male presence. There had never been another man. "Just" her best-friend/lover/roommate, who was always there for her. Did he just expect them to take up again, as if nothing happened? And what about Omid?

Had he been imprisoned? Disfigured like her from the blast? Did he have amnesia for a while? The possibilities raced through her head as she sat immobilized in the car. Cool morning air rushed in around her carrying the bustling sounds of Paris in the morning.

"Mom?" Yasmeen held out her hand to help Anoush up. "It'll be OK."

Anoush allowed herself to be guided out of the taxi and stood blinking outside the iconic glass pyramid.

The three stepped inside; the dim interior blinding them momentarily. Tourists buzzed and swarmed like bees in the lobby. The three bought their tickets and followed the map Yasmeen procured to find the Persian Section, passing wide-eyed visitors with upturned faces, raptly absorbed in their audio narratives. Tahj skipped alongside, eager to meet his grandfather.

A magnificent arch opened to the Persian Wing, guarded by two winged bulls bearing the head of a bearded king crowned with a cylindrical headdress. They passed into the somewhat darkened, cavernous hall that held the first exhibits. From a bench, a figure rose and approached. Dimples, wavy brown hair in an Elvis

hairstyle and a brilliant smile greeted them as Mirza appeared before them like an apparition, gazing longingly at Anoush, and then joyfully at Yasmeen and Tahj. He looked just fifteen years older than when they were in college.

Anoush broke the silence.

"You're still *young*! How can this be?" she croaked, losing all composure as she began trembling uncontrollably, hands forming fists.

Mirza's eyes filled with tears as his hand raised to touch Anoush's disfigured face. She shrunk back slightly, but allowed it.

"My jasmine blossom," he whispered and with that Anoush threw herself into his arms, sobbing. Yasmeen and Tahj joined in the hug, until a guard appeared, worried that something was wrong.

When at last they were able to separate, Mirza cleared his throat.

"I have a lot to tell you. Come, let's sit down."

"This is your daughter Yasmeen and your grandson Tahj," Anoush pronounced carefully, suddenly much more grounded. "How about we start with this...I am 64 and you are...?"

"36, apparently."

Tahj looked up at Mirza with big brown eyes and grinned, "Pleased to meet you...uh, Grandpa. Why don't you look like a Granpa?"

He turned to Yasmeen, "Does this make Grandma a cougar?"

The three adults burst in laughter, easing the tension that had filled the room.

What was Lost is Found

What was Lost is Found

❧ 23 ❧

The Louvre, Persian Wing

Mirza, Anoush, Yasmeen, and Tahj sat on a bench facing a large frieze of five Persian archers striding across a turquoise background. The archers wore gold headbands and gold patterned tunics and each carried a spear before them like a staff.

"I was in a hospital, then a prison for nearly four years," Mirza began. "Solitary."

"The only thing that kept me sane was the company I had in my cell. Yes, I know I just said I was in solitary. By my third year, I started noticing little eyes in the shadows, so I'd hide a few bread crumbs in my pocket at dinner, and later leave them out for the mouse. I began having monologues with it, realizing that if anyone overheard, they'd put me in a straitjacket for sure. Or not. It's not like anyone cared what happened to me.

"So I'm talking to the mouse one night, rambling on about the life I'd had and how I miss everyone I used to know. Suddenly, from about where the eyes are, low to the floor, a voice clearly says, 'So, you wanna get outta here, or what?'

"After nearly jumping out of my skin, I thought perhaps a neighboring cellmate might be playing tricks on me, but it was late at night. When I peeked out the grate at the top of my cell door, it looked like everyone was asleep. And from the sound of all the snoring, my whispers to a mouse in my cell would hardly wake anyone up.

"So I sit down on my bed, take a deep breath and look into the shadows; the hair on the back of my neck raised and all."

"Well? What'll it be? You wanna rot in here the rest of yer life, or come with me somewhere else?"

"'Where?' I find myself asking, even though I know I'm taking one step farther from sanity as I do. I mean, a monologue with a mouse is one thing, but this one's answering me..."

"Where ya wanna go?"

"'California,' I say, deciding to be decisive. I just yanked the word out of the air. California seems safe, and light years away from this hellhole. A place where I might not get punched or shot at as often as I could here."

"You're in luck, my friend...that's a place I can take you."

"Suddenly I realize I know nothing about this creature.

"'Excuse me...I don't mean to be impolite, but who are you? *What* are you?' I ask, cringing inwardly at how rude I sound.

"With that, the eyes rise to about two feet off the ground, and start advancing out of the shadow. Now, I've got some serious willies. A tiny man stands before me, the size of a toddler. He's oddly dressed, like a character out of a medieval European tale: leather jerkin, cape, metal epaulets that look like lions, so his arms are emerging from the mouths of the cats. With long, curly brown hair and a beard, his warriorlike appearance is softened by dozens of crinkles in his nut brown face that appear with his broad smile. Judging by his laugh lines it looks like he smiles a lot. He removes his winged helmet and takes a grand bow, 'Aylard the Terrible, at your service'."

"'Mirza', I nod, trying not to laugh, as he seems anything but terrible. I'm not sure whether I should offer my hand to shake, but reach down anyway to clasp his tiny mitt. He has a firm grip for one so small.

"Listen, Aylard, I'm really grateful for your offer, but I'm curious...why would you want to help me?

"You left regular offerings and gave me stories. Stories are very valuable among my people. A kind of currency. You were respectful. That's a rarity between humans and my kind. And also, you can see me."

"No disrespect intended, but...what is your kind?" I asked.

"We are the Hidden People. Some of you would call us trolls, but we find the term derogatory and politically incorrect," Aylard replied. "Our origins are earlier than those of mankind, and at a certain point, coexisting on Earth with humans remaining aware of us just resulted in our slaughter. So we raised our vibration and became invisible to the eye...of most," he finished.

"After the 'politically incorrect' statement, I don't dare tell him I'd thought he was a mouse."

"'So...you in or out?' he taps his wrist where a watch would be."

"I consider his offer. What do I have to lose?

"'When can we go?' I ask."

"'Right now, if you like.' With that he beckons me closer, turns and then pushes on the far wall. A two-foot high slice of it swings away from him; a child-sized door. I see green beyond the stone frame and smell rich loamy earth and pine needles. Sunlight streams into my cell. The distant scree of a red-tailed hawk brings tears to my

eyes. I've been deprived of fresh air and sunshine for so long. The raptor's piercing cry is the very sound of freedom!

"In a heartbeat I'm crawling through after him. I hear the door thunk closed behind me.

"'Don't look back!' he shouts just as my head begins to swivel.

"I rise to my feet. And raise my eyes to an outdoor cathedral of redwood trees. The soft tinkling of a stream caresses my ears, like the sound of a thousand diamonds tumbling over one another. It's been so long since I've been in nature, I don't think I've ever heard anything sweeter.

"A cool breeze soughs through branches overhead. Sunlight filters golden through an endless thatch of branches. My feet dig into a pine-needle carpet. I inhale deeply the clear, clean smell of the forest, raise my hands in joy, and then silently bring them to my heart, closing my eyes. The first peace I've known in ages fills me completely.

~

"My shoulder is bumped, and I open my eyes to see a group of teenage hippie kids walking past me, eyeing my prison uniform warily. 'Sorry,' one of them says. They shrug at my deer in the headlights expression and continue on, carrying walking sticks and backpacks and sharing a doobie amongst themselves.

"'Hey, where am I?' I call after them.

"The kid holding the roach turns around and shakes his head, 'Aw man, you must've got hold of some bad shit. Bummer.' He offers his reefer, and dazed, I take a puff.

"'Thanks, man,' I say."

The Louvre, Persian Wing

"'Keep it,' the kid says, 'you need it more than me. You're in San Geronimo. California. Roy's Redwoods. Would you like the year?'

"Why not?"

"2015."

"I nod sagely. Try not to freak out. Consider all of this as the hikers walk away. I can hear their conversation. 'Remember the time we found those brownies in Ellie's old man's fridge, and scarfed them all down? We thought we were going to die!' This cracks them all up as they disappear around a bend.

"I salute them with the remains of the fatty and begin wandering among the trees."

"Pssst!"

"*Wha?* I see no one around."

"'Psssst!! It's coming from inside a nearby tree. I walk around the magnificent trunk and see that the tree is hollow. Aylard pokes his head out and waves me in.

"'Did you just disappear when those kids arrived and beam yourself into this tree?' I say."

"Something like that,' Aylard answers with a Cheshire Cat smirk.

"I step down a foot below the forest floor into a cozy cave within the tree and sit down cross-legged next to my new companion.

"'What're ya doing talking to people?' he scolds. 'You're lucky they were just some stoner hippie kids! We need to get you some new duds and educate you about your new home....and maybe get

you a shave,' he considers my sizeable beard which matches his in exuberance. 'That is, unless you want to join the local commune?'"

"'Uh, maybe?' I stammer.

"Aylard's hands flutter before my face and I'm suddenly feeling very sleepy.

"'Rest here a while," he says, as I nod obediently and black out on a bed of pine needles.

"When I wake, he's gone and it's dark. *Now what?* I climb out of the redwood bowl and head over to the stream. The smoke has given me a raging thirst. I just lay down at the water's edge and gulp and gulp like a savage, until I hear..."

""Leave some for the fish,' in a big, boomy voice from high above.

"I freeze and rise slowly, looking all around me. No one.

"We get salmon spawning in this creek every year. With all your gulping, I'd be surprised if you haven't swallowed a fry or two."

"'Who's there?' I ask, not sure where to run or hide.

"'Roy.' The voice floats down to me from the treetops. 'And by the way...you're standing on me.'"

"I look down and jump.

"Long roots from all directions converge into twin redwoods that rise, then join, where they're flanked by giant... hands...on hips.

"I blink and sure enough, high in the tree canopy an enormous head nods, accompanied by the sound of branches and leaves

fluttering. He raises an immense hand and waves down to me affably."

"'Found me,' he says in that avuncular, patient voice of his."

"You're Roy?"

"'Yep, and this grove is my family.' He swivels his head proudly and takes in the neighbors, branches swishing.

"I consider the other trees, but they look like redwoods, not giant tree people.

"'How come you have a face and hands and the others don't?' I wonder aloud."

"We don't reveal ourselves to humans often, but Aylard told me your story, so I made an exception. Also, I am an Ent, a more evolved member of my community, so I have more capabilities than my relatives...not that I'm any better than them mind you," he added rather nervously as he looked around.

"Just then a neighboring tree bent and swished its topmost branches into Roy's head. There was no wind.

"'Ow! I said I wasn't any better than you...!' he whined. Then he composed himself, as only a 300 foot redwood can."

"Please...sit....And you are?"

"Mirza."

"'Please, sit, Mirza.' Roy beckons and I carefully select a rock by the stream and settle into getting to know my first talking tree."

The Louvre, Persian Wing

"'So, first, you must know that Ents can move, Roy begins, and to my amazement, starts making worrisome creaking and splintering sounds as he bends where knees would be and sits down facing me. The resounding thud of his woody butt hitting the Earth shakes the forest like a small earthquake.

"'I know... I know...' Roy sighs, looking up into the thatch of treetops. 'Show off.' He shrugs and turns his attention back to me."

"Weed's gotten a lot stronger since college, I decided."

~

"On a clothesline down the road, just beyond Les Deau Oiseaux restaurant, a farmer's overalls and red plaid shirt flap, forgotten in the night. Standing atop the nearby dog house, in which the bewitched pit bull snores, Aylard tugs the line, reeling the clothing toward himself. A tie-dyed T shirt and some scruffy jeans hang near them. He pulls them off. Bunching them under his arm, he scurries into the night. Spotting the farmer's shoes outside the front door he blesses his luck. This is Marin after all, and even farmer's houses are shoeless houses...a practice trolls find laughable, with the constant chill of the Bay Area. Aylard snags the boots as well and sprints back to Roy's Redwoods.

~

By now, Tahj was sitting on the floor in front of Mirza in the Louvre, cross legged and mouth agape. Yasmeen sat beside him with her arm on his shoulder. Anoush just sat in shock by Mirza's side, eyes never leaving his face, and worrying that she was lucky to only have an outer manifestation from the blast.

~

The Louvre, Persian Wing

"I wake curled on the sweet-smelling pine needle bed, inside the same redwood where I'd fallen asleep. Aylard sits at the opening, contemplatively puffing an odd, long-stemmed pipe. He turns to me, 'So, the sleepyhead is finally awake,' he chuckles.

"'I met Roy...I think.' I say to Aylard as I rub my eyes and stretch.

"'Roy likes to introduce himself to people under...unusual circumstances,' Aylard winked. 'Don't worry, though...If he chose to reveal himself to you while I was gone, you really did meet him.'"

"Whew!" I sigh, sitting up.

"'Oh, by the way, your new wardrobe is there,' Aylard points to a neatly folded pile inside the redwood tree.

"When I emerge in the tie-died T shirt and jeans moments later, Aylard appraises me carefully.

"'Perfect!' he declares. 'Now we need to mainstream you. Let's go visit my friend Chickpea.'"

The Louvre, Persian Wing

❧ 24 ☙

Chickpea

Puzzled, Mirza nonetheless followed Aylard on a hike through Roy's trails for about a mile or so. The path opened out onto a farm.

"Drip Irrigation and Solar Panels, m'boy, it's all the rage," Aylard enthused as he pointed to a large sign by the barn that read,

Burnside Solar and Irrigation

As they approached the barn, chickens scattered and a 60-something compact man with a wizened face and twinkling eyes stepped out and greeted them.

"Mirza, Chickpea. Chickpea, Mirza."

Chickpea tipped his straw Farmer Bob hat and squinted at the new arrival.

"Another rescue?"

"Yep. So, whaddaya think, Chick? Need an extra hand around hear?"

Chickpea rubbed his stubble, cocked his head, then squinted into the sun, seeming to make some obscure calculations. He slapped his thigh.

The Secret of the Cylinder

"Hell, wouldn't you know it? I was just complaining to the wife that I was getting a little old to do this all by myself. Suppose he'll need a place to stay too?"

"If it's not too much trouble, sir," Mirza responded.

"Why not?!" Chickpea roared. See that outbuilding over there?" He pointed down the rolling landscape to a small cottage perched at the edge of a grove of olive trees.

Mirza nodded.

"I assume this'll be W2?" Chickpea deadpanned.

Mirza looked to Aylard, confused. The two locals guffawed. Aylard did a little circular stompy dance as he laughed. Chickpea slapped his thigh again.

"I'm just yankin' yer chain," Chickpea chuckled. "I pay cash every two weeks. If I like yer work you get a raise in a month."

Mirza brightened.

"Know how to drive a tractor?"

"No sir."

"Well, then, what's takin' you so long? Get up on that thing and I'll show you how."

Mirza turned to thank Aylard.

But he was gone.

~

Chickpea

"So how do you know Aylard," Mirza asked Chickpea before taking a big bite of turkey wrap.

He and Chickpea were resting at a job site in the shade of an enormous Live Oak. Before them it looked like gophers had gone wild — an entire backyard was dug up into long, shallow trenches. Lengths of PVC pipe lay in a stack nearby.

"Mmmmmm....I guess it must have been Beltane, 2000." Chickpea munched thoughtfully; a dreamy look in his eye.

"That's when I became a true believer in my grandmother's stories."

Mirza nodded encouragingly.

"I was born in Scotland, and my grandmother told me many stories about the Little People when I was quite small. She would always leave a saucer of milk and a little bread out for them at night. My mother would roll her eyes and say, "Pish posh! Such nonsense, ma. You go putting ideas like that into his head, he'll believe cats can fiddle."

"But I knew they were real. Had a little friend meself. I only talked with my grandmother about Elnaril. He was a wee one who would appear by my bedside whenever I was lonely or frightened at night. He'd tell me the funniest stories and fall asleep with me. I always woke up alone, but comforted.

"But boys grow up and by the time I was in school I'd quite forgotten about Elnaril, having new school chums of my own to pal around with.

"Then, fifteen years ago, a widower of five years, I decided I would be lonely no more and joined some friends at a Beltane ritual. It

was a bittersweet day, bringing back memories of my laughing Mary Kate and the times we'd twined the ribbons round the Maypole ourselves. And then how we'd bless the garden and do some planting of our own in the fields afterwards; making love under the stars. I can still smell the flowery fragrance of her lovely blonde curls, he sighed. Anyway, that Beltane, because of all the memories it brought up, I had a little too much mead after the ceremony and got lost walking in the woods back to my house. I'd just decided to pray I wouldn't freeze, and found me a hallowed out Redwood with a nice pine needle-covered floor.

When I woke the next morning, this Wee One was just sitting there not two feet away, considering me, smoking an odd pipe.

"Elnaril!" I said joyously. "You found me, my old friend."

His eyes sparkled and he said, "No, human. I am not your childhood friend. He deigned not to cross the ocean and leave his homeland as you did. But he's instructed me to look after you."

And so he did—feeding me, introducing me to Roy, pointing me in the right direction to get back home. He even gave me a nasty potion that cured my hangover. Never gave me the recipe, no matter how many times I asked. I owed him a huge favor.

"And so the favor was repaid," Mirza said humbly. "I'm honored to be part of this circle of reciprocity."

❧ 25 ❧

Reunion

Mirza glanced at his audience and realized he'd been talking a long time. Too long for mouths to stay open like that.

"Fast forward to 2021 and I'm in my cottage a few nights ago. I see the Nobel awards on TV and learn the truth that you'd not only lived but succeeded in our mission! I'd been told you were dead when they threw me in prison and my life was over.

"After many calls to various offices of the committee, I was able to convince someone of the truth of our history and they gave me your contact information. I flew to Paris immediately, not even knowing whether you'd see me. But I'm so grateful you agreed to…"

"I came through the portal into the future and only started aging from the point at which I arrived on the other side."

Anoush hadn't broken eye contact with Mirza the entire story, but now she noticed his left eye trailing off.

"Did you lose your eye in the blast?" she asked softly.

"Yes," he replied. "But that's a loss I can mostly hide."

Anoush reached her hand out and covered his heart. "What about this one?" Mirza teared up and placed his hand over Anoush's.

The Secret of the Cylinder

Yasmeen and Tahj had been watching the exchange silently and now leapt over to hug Mirza.

"You're coming home with us, Dad. For good!" Yasmeen pronounced.

~

A block away from the Louvre, Sorouch Zare lies in wait. He attaches a silencer to his gun and moves closer to a wall so he can see the exit of the museum. He steadies his arm against the brick surface and takes aim. "Once and for all," he mutters darkly. *I didn't think that last trick of yours was funny at all...having your shapeshifter friend go out shopping as you. It was only after I'd followed her into an alley and grabbed her that she transformed back into your cursed college roommate and escaped me. I've been biding my time for five years...*

Behind him, he hears the click of a trigger being cocked. "Sorouch Zare, put the gun down," barks a SWAT team soldier. Sorouch swings around, gun pointed to fire wildly, but before he can pump off a round, his body is pounded with the spray of Interpol bullets.

~

The family began walking slowly through the many rooms of the Persian Exhibit. Suddenly, Anoush stiffened.

"Stop right there!" she said to Mirza.

He looked at her worriedly and stopped. Yasmeen let out a gasp when she saw what her mother was looking at. Behind Mirza was a mosaic of Belshazaar the 2nd. While not resembling Mirza's face, the figure held the same pose Mirza stood in right now.

"And look there!" Anoush gasped. Several feet away was a carving of a merman with a beard and domed hat. "That was in my parent's house in Basra," she said. "I don't know how I know, but I do! It was one of my favorite carvings." She raced over it and began stroking it, setting off the proximity alarm. A guard came over and warned her. She apologized and they moved on.

"Not my parents from *this* life," she began, trailing off, by way of awkward explanation.

"It's hard to look at anything the same way, now, isn't it?"

Mirza smiled, putting his arm around Anoush's shoulders and attracting the calculating stares of several people. *Is he her son or her lover?* Noticing them, he kissed her on the lips and winked to the busybodies, causing a mother to gasp and hurry her child away.

He leaned over and whispered in Anoush's ear, "Now I'll be your younger man, for as long as you'll have me."

She blushed, giggled and nuzzled her head into his shoulder as they left the museum with Yasmeen and Tahj.

"I'll have you forever, my love."

~

The Interpol's alarm sounds its two toned blare just down the street. Anoush and Mirza don't pay it any attention; eyes only for each other.

"Ah, the sound of freedom," Yasmeen quips, making Tahj laugh as he skips alongside his family.

Reunion

❧ 26 ☙

Bonus Story – Once Felt, Never Forgotten

On the Road to Bhakti…A Pilgrimage to the Virgin of Guadalupe in Mexico City

(First published in Indie Shaman Magazine, London, Issue 17, Summer 2013)

"This your first pilgrimage?" I stage-whispered to a gal from my group. She giggled and nodded. After four hours of solemn shuffling alongside men carrying large framed images of the Virgin Mary lashed to their backs, my lapsed Catholic inner child was feeling mischievous. Monty Python mischievous.

In my 20 years of practicing yoga, I'd never understood why people took pilgrimages. Then a significant relationship in my life ended. I needed introspection and some divine assistance. The much-prophesied Solstice seemed like the perfect time, so I traveled to Mexico City and joined seven million fellow pilgrims for an eight-hour odyssey.

~

Before we set off for our evening trek, I'd fretted over what to bring. Traveling light was a priority. Paranoid of pickpockets, I debated leaving my camera in the hotel safe as I stashed only enough money for taxi fare in my bra.

My roommate eyed me worriedly as she neatly laid out a matching TravelSmith outfit on her bed, "Did you know that at the 1954 Kumbh Mela pilgrimage in India, 500 people were killed in a stampede?"

"Um, no...," I blurted. I hadn't considered claustrophobia or crowd crushing until just then. Suddenly it was 1985...

I'd arrived at the Providence (Rhode Island) Civic Center for a Kool and the Gang concert, and stood with other earlybirds by the closed glass doors to the auditorium. The crowd swelled significantly as showtime neared. Suddenly, far from me, a single door opened. The throng surged, lifting me off my feet and pinning me like a bug against a glass wall. Panic and utter helplessness washed over me as the glass gave, but thankfully did not break...And then other doors opened and my primal fear subsided as I stumbled in with the herd to see the show.

~

As we began our hike in Tlaltelolco—site of the Templo Mayor, one of the main Aztec temples—our trip leader gave us each a pack of six black and six white stones. Over the course of our walk he instructed us to assign each rock various traumas we'd experienced in childhood or at each milestone in our life. These were our prayer beads to ponder and worry throughout the evening, as we considered the things that held us back in our lives. The stones would be offered at the basilica, our destination, and the Virgin would release from us the heavy energy associated with these traumas—mending the holes in our souls—in a simple but elegant syncretism of faiths.

Bonus Story - Once Felt, Never Forgotten

~

Hanging low and swollen in the sky, a vermillion Jupiter was the first of many celestial wonders that night—the perfect lantern to light our way, as we hiked for seven miles from 7 p.m. to 3 a.m. on 12/12/12. It limned our passage to the ancient Temple of Tonantzin Coatlicue—Mother Earth and Goddess of Life and Death. The temple was destroyed by the Spanish and rebuilt into the original chapel for the Virgin of Guadalupe.

~

"Don't turn down anything people give you!" my trip leader instructed. "You'll hurt their feelings, and these gifts are offered from the kindness of their hearts."

My first present was a card handed to me by a calm smiling man. This being my first boon, I felt excited as a kid who'd fished out the Cracker Jack prize. The card bore an image of the Virgin of Guadalupe on one side, and a prayer to her on the other.

Soon, however, my growling stomach reminded me that I hadn't had dinner. With a pang, I noticed a young couple from our group to my left holding SANDWICHES. They seemed to be debating whether they dared eat them or not. I craned my neck left to right like a starving baby bird, but soon became distracted by a 40-something local man dragging a wooden box by a rope with a rapt look on his face. The regular appearance of men toting four foot crosses on their shoulders—complete with grim Jesus—also took my mind off my tummy. It was lucky that I forgot about the treats so near and yet so far, because food was not to find its way to me that night. I would arrive at our destination in proper fasted form…

Bonus Story - Once Felt, Never Forgotten

At one point my food radar caused me to be in a perplexing place. Without thinking, I'd accepted a very full cup of black coffee that…I realized a second later, I didn't want. As I hurried to rejoin my group, the obsidian liquid sloshed dangerously close to the edge. The coffee giver had so enthusiastically proffered his gift, and with the trip leader's directive drumming through my head…how could I refuse? I debated being rude to the tradition… What would HAPPEN if someone threw away their boon? I considered my options. Cups, wrappers, and all manifestations of trash were piled high on the sidewalk to my right and left. Dumping the liquid in the street simply wasn't an option—I would've wetted many pilgrim toes…including mine. My San Francisco recycler mentality agonized over the spec of litter I'd be adding to the tonnage that lay strewn everywhere. I finally found a space on the sidewalk to set down the brimming cup, and bounded guiltily onward.

~

Over time, the parade my group had merged with bottlenecked from a 20-shoulder-across street to a 5-across pedestrian walkway in the middle of an avenue. Diminutive police officers stood on bollards lining the thin causeway every 10 feet, providing a constant presence. The gateway to the Vegas-lit basilica complex allowed just three-shoulders-across entry. Once inside, we were reduced to a singular serpentine shuffle.

~

Inside the compound, the press of devout seekers covered every square inch of pavement. I stepped carefully over the feet of family after family camped out on the steps of the church, clearly

exhausted after their long trek from their home village (some had walked for months). Not a single baby cried among seven million pilgrims. My mind staggered with the enormity of that many hushed children…and where were the bathrooms?

A trust and gentleness pervaded as families slept atop blankets they'd placed on sidewalks, stairs and street corners….any place out of the immediate flow of foot traffic.

I soon realized my earlier paranoia of pickpockets, stampedes, and crowd crushing was totally unfounded, as all the men I passed, bumped into, or witnessed were peaceful, reverent, and deferential. I was never pushed or regarded suggestively the entire evening.

~

We climbed up to the Temple of Tonantzin Coatlique, past Virgin dioramas one could pose by for pictures. At the top we were greeted by domed rooftops and breathtaking views of the snaking streets below feeding the devout into the basilica. Joining the rapt, upturned faces of the faithful, I entered the chapel. A sweet, light energy filled the high-ceilinged edifice, which was tiled in blue and white and bursting with flowers. The circa 16th century statuary backed by suns, moons and stars—and especially the Virgin statue, sitting atop a crescent moon and containing complex indigenous spiritual symbolism that our trip leader had explained to us—pleased my inner Pagan greatly.

I exited into the strobe-illuminated night to see fireworks create a number "7" in the sky…Aztec symbol of healing. With that auspicious omen, I tossed my stones over a low stone wall, beyond which was a grassy hillside—sending my prayers, and my traumas to the Mother's healing. I descended the stairs. At the base of the

old Temple, I felt suddenly washed with a lightness and release. It reminded me of *hucha mikuy*, the Peruvian shamanic method of transforming heavy energy into light, refined energy. Or, if you like, the transubstantiation performed with a chalice at either a pagan ritual or a Christian mass.

As we milled slowly around the main basilica yard in the out-stream, I followed many pilgrim arms pointing to the heavens and gasped. Hovering low and large over the modern basilica, soundlessly flashing a green oval of lights, then a white one was something extremely non-ordinary. Occasionally the specter darted with impossible speed to the right or left. It seemed to be studying this epicenter of human empathy for its uniqueness and beauty in stark contrast to all the other nastiness on the planet; hovering for the longest time over the basilica. I blinked and it was gone.

My gaze traveled to the gold-framed, original *tilma* in the modern basilica—the cape of Juan Diego—to whom the Virgin had appeared, and with which he had carried the impossible Castillian roses at the Virgin's request to the local church, to validate his vision. The image of Mary had remained on the cape when he shook the roses out. In 1951 photographers discovered a reflection in the Virgin's eyes, which on magnification, revealed all 14 witnesses present when the *tilma* was first revealed to the padre in 1531, including a small family. Interestingly, Hernán Cortés, the conquistador who overthrew the Aztec Empire in 1521, was from Extremadura, Spain, home to Our Lady of Guadalupe, Extremadura—one of three black Madonnas in Spain. Was her well-timed Mexican appearance a political move or a miracle? The *tilma* has not been studied scientifically since 1982.

~

Bonus Story - Once Felt, Never Forgotten

Our return trek created a feeling of expansiveness as personal space once again emerged. The inbound crowd became threadier and younger, more exuberant; many of them high-fiving or waving to the tall men in our group who were risking loss of blood to limbs by maintaining upraised arms to signal our group's edges, and not lose any weary trekkers.

~

Later that day, back at the hotel room and after some much-needed rest, I unrolled my yoga mat and flicked on some kirtan music. Suddenly, just a few notes into the first song, exquisite ecstasy flooded my body like a megadose of endorphins… And I got it… Why people take pilgrimages. That same vibration can be triggered so easily afterwards! My heart expanded as if an inner sun were shining within me. I began my Ujayyi breathing and let the feeling deepen as I stretched into my first pose… grateful for such incredible beauty in the midst of such unassuming pilgrims.

Once felt, it is never forgotten.

Bonus Story - Once Felt, Never Forgotten

❧ 27 ☙

Bonus Story - Me and my Shadow

Did the Mayans get it Wrong? What's Next?

We survived the Solstice. The end of the world. I wasn't particularly surprised. Were you? Long before that fateful day, I learned about a different calendar that allows us to live much longer. Because it looks like we're still here.

I refer to the Aztec calendar, the image that we most associate with the Mayan calendar. But unlike the Mayan's, and just like a Timex, the Aztec calendar keeps on ticking...beyond the much-prophesied Solstice. Not only that, but the Aztec calendar—and the indigenous wisdom behind it—holds clues to how our future will unfold. And how to ready ourselves for this new era called the Sixth Sun.

~

As a cross-cultural shamanic practitioner, specializing in soul retrieval, I've explored many wisdom streams to arrive at my current toolkit. The Toltec/Aztec path has some very special practices to help us deal with the full range of human foibles, when we're faced with upcoming challenges unique to this Sixth Sun.

~

Me and my Shadow

I first learned about this Sixth Sun from Aztec/Toltec teacher Sergio Magaña Ocelocoyotl (coyote jaguar). A brilliant and eloquent young man, Sergio expertly bridges the modern world with that of his indigenous teachers and ancestors. There is no surprise that he was born with both Castilian and indigenous blood in his veins. He shares practices that align us with ancient, universal rhythms, which can evoke deep, positive change in our lives…*if we do the work.*

He has been teaching in Mexico for over twelve years, and in the US and Europe since 2010. Sergio has learned from great masters in the Mexica lineage including Aztec Anubis, Xolotl José Luis Chávez Martínez, keeper of the ancient Nahuatl wisdom; Xolotl's wife Alma, teacher of the feminine mysteries—healing with obsidian tools and the *popochcomitl*, or copal burner; and Hugo Nahui, a gifted scholar on stellar events and their impact on our lives.

I was one of the lucky few who was able to attend an authentic ceremony in Mexico on the auspicious date of 12/21/12. Not many also knew that at the Solstice there was a time of no time where the Universe stood still and opportunity was possible. Picture this…

I am near the Zocalo (main square) in Mexico City in ceremony officiated by Xolotl and his priestess wife, Alma. It is the eight seconds of no-time at 5:13 a.m. The circle is suddenly hushed. One hundred people, from all points of the globe, power out to the universe our big intentions for ourselves, our families, countries and planet, as the Sixth Sun dawns. A warm, tingly energy pours out from my heart. I feel hugely expansive and peaceful, like time did stop and anything was possible—perhaps we were changing the world in that very moment. When the eight seconds were over, we resume our frenzied dancing as hummingbirds, eagles, and macaws; miming the expert moves of native celebrants, and calling in all they represent.

~

Yet that was but a moment in time that marked an official goodbye to an old way of being and ushered in the influence of the next "Sun", the Sixth Sun. Each Era spans 6,625 years. While the Fifth Sun was an era of outer conquest and seeking wisdom and happiness in the world around us, the Sixth Sun ushers in an era of inner listening—of working with the wisdom within—and deepens until it is in full control on 12/21/2021.

In other words, this is a time of reckoning with our shadow: those cast-off parts of ourselves that we have buried away from our conscious awareness. Those things we hide from ourselves. Often it is because of trauma that we push both our gifts and negative experiences away from the light. Qualities like insecurity, or jealousy—or even a talent for singing that never gets expressed for fear of public humiliation—these things cause us pain. The shadow can be positive as well as negative, and can help as well as hinder us. Unfortunately, we usually end up acting out aspects of our shadow when they are repressed, such as criticizing the successful artist. When others exhibit our shadow qualities, we often have strong negative feelings toward these people, but never consider why this might be. It is because they are expressing disowned aspects of ourselves.

The Aztec/Toltec tradition that Sergio presents helps people to realize that, yes, we ALL have a shadow, whether we deny it or not. This is nothing to be ashamed of; it is a human condition. Uniquely, this tradition provides tools, such as the Obsidian Mirror, for actually making a connection—seeing, feeling, creating awareness, and ownership—of the 15 aspects of the shadow—positive and negative—that the tradition recognized and urges us to work with. And then, if one chooses, and with commitment and discipline, they can transform the harmful aspects of their shadow to helpful ones. Turning one's own worst enemy into their inner hero. Becoming more effective in one's life. The life-affirming effects are similar to those gained through soul retrieval or other

more traditional psychotherapy methods that also work with dissociation.

Why is it important to acknowledge and transform our shadow NOW? Because we live in accelerated times. Even more so, after 12/21/12. Our thoughts and actions manifest much more quickly now. This is one of the aspects of the Sixth Sun Era, an era of "endarkenment". We can create heaven or hell on this Earth much easier now. The cosmos is assisting us. It is our choice which of the two we'd like to create in our life. The "easy" path is to give in to inner darkness—react without thinking, say something off the top of our head because it's a popular sentiment, but not something that's been thought through as to whether it really rings true in our heart. The challenge is to rise above our "pain body" (as Eckhart Tolle calls it) of ourselves, our family, our culture, or our country and shed light on our inner darkness. And in so doing, bring more light and hope to the human condition at this point in time. When it is so desperately needed.

~

I was terrified to look at my shadow…as anyone would be…but knew it was my responsibility. I'd worked with it before, but like peeling an onion, found there were always more layers. Luckily, I was offered an opportunity to work on mine in Mexico at an auspicious moment in time. A significant relationship in my life had just unraveled and ended. Additionally, I'd been experiencing the disorientation of hot flashes, weight gain, hormonal fluctuations, and most significantly, an urgency to address my inner victim—to no longer put up with people and situations in my life that were not in integrity. That were not congruent with the path of dignity I needed to walk. I couldn't tell whether what I'd been experiencing were growing pains, ascension symptoms, or something else, but I wanted to set some awareness and healing in motion by refocusing my attention in ritual and connection with

the Earth. To make sense—in a shamanic setting—of the changes in my life. What better place to do this than the energetic center of Mexico at this time in history?

~

I sit cross-legged in a temazcal, *or sweat lodge, also led by Xolotl and Alma. We are on one of many islands dotting the canals of Xochimilco (place of flowers); one of the original parts of Mexico City.*

Unlike the Solstice ritual, this temazcal *is a very intimate, personal affair. Our lodge is a green reed dome, partially covered by tarps. Clad in sarongs, shorts, and skivvies, our group of 20 crawls to their places inside, as an eagle circles overhead under a clear blue dome—an auspicious omen.*

As the couple's preteen girl and boy play on the grassy lawn outside, I feel like we become the couple's 20 children as their gentle ministrations are translated from Spanish to English...but soon realize, that here, in the temazcal, *we are children of Earth parents who possess deep, healing love and also claws and fangs.*

Since I'd participated in over half a dozen sweatlodges already, fear of the unknown had long vanished with my initial one. Here, I eagerly anticipated the hermetic hug of the warm, dark womb. I was joyful for the opportunity to step between the worlds, and outside of everyday life...something I hadn't done in a while.

~

Introductions are made, and the womb-like space feels initially safe and cozy. The first round of red hot stones is pitchforked in; each rock cradled by very long, sharp tines that slide inches from my bare leg. I release my

Bonus Story - Me and my Shadow

breath when the final stone is placed, blessed, and the door closed. Because I'd requested a personal healing for bronchitis, Xolotl now ushers me to sit by the central fire pit, facing away from it. It's a chill, windy day outside, and I'm happy to abandon my drafty seat by the door. He sprinkles water on the stones.

Luxuriating in the enveloping steam bath, I'm now feeling held by my surrogate parents. Sighing deeply, I relax into the comforting silence. Then...surprise! My back is whipped with a leafy tree branch! I feel...oddly Catholic and almost laugh. The leaves don't hurt, but an occasional spark singes my skin for a microsecond. Had he touched the branch to the stones first?! Was my hair going to burn?! I just had it done!

As gifted shamans, my "parents" know what they are doing. The temazcal balances health, mind and emotions. Sometimes certain plants are used to enhance the work and help the client with their inner struggle to change; in particular Pirul (Pepper Plant), Rosemary, and Santa Maria (Spearmint). *The practitioner asks the stones of the* temazcal *for balance and healing — touching them briefly with the herb — and then taps the affected area on the client with the plant.* Xolotl and Alma believe sickness is caused by unbalanced energy; resulting in chemical, physical, social, biological, and mind alterations. *Their methods to rebalance a person include* temazcal, infusions, massage, cleansings, dancing, and breathing exercises. Most importantly, as in other shamanic healing methods, faith assists the success of the client's inner work.

With each touch of the pepper branch, I feel a fluttering inside my chest of dark wings, echoing those of the eagle overhead. Shards of old grief, long buried, begin to surface. I gasp, cough, and weep.

A couple hours later I emerge from the lodge, absolutely radiant — my lungs and skin gloriously clear and hydrated. Purified for the Solstice ceremony and respectful of Xolotl and Alma's Earth parent power.

Bonus Story – Me and my Shadow

~

It was only much later, as I assimilated all the work we did, that I realized my personal growing pains simply mirrored those of Mother Earth. The angst of this awareness wrenched my heart and made me feel a powerful, yet tender responsibility for both her and myself. Wise new actions were and continue to be called for. In some cases these actions involve culling—with intention—the things that no longer contribute to the well-being of either my life or that of the planet.

We are birthing our new selves for this new era, as we agonize together with the contractions, like Inanna comforting Ereshkigel in the underworld—stepping into our darkness, forsaking our outer self-centered trappings of beauty or security or being the superstar lone wolf…because it is called for. Not knowing whether we'll be dismembered by the process, or whether—like Osiris—we'll be missing a part of ourselves when the journey is over; but knowing that surely we will be transformed. All the while we are being forged and tempered into swords of better discernment, in the cave, in our *chicomostoc*, our cauldron of transformation. Grappling with our shadow. Stepping into our portal to great power.

It's time to seize our inner swords. To become better stewards of both our shadow…and the planet. We are being called… This is what's next.

Sergio says, "We are entering the cycle of the Obsidian Eagle, a place where our dreams and our enlightenment are attained through the path of darkness, through the transformation of our own cave (shadow)."

Ometeotl. (And so it is!)

Bonus Story - Me and my Shadow

ଓଃ 28 ଽ୦

Bonus Story – The Cosmic Dynamo

A New Toltec Teaching Revealed for the Sixth Sun

(Adapted from an article published in Indie Shaman Magazine, London, Issue 16, Spring 2013)

As a cross-cultural shamanic practitioner, I've explored many wisdom streams over the years of my practice to arrive at my current toolkit. In all my studies, however, I've never heard of a Cosmic Dynamo, something I directly experienced on the Solstice of 2012. This ancient teaching, revealed to the outside world for the first time, works with vastly powerful Earth forces to disseminate blessings to individuals, families, countries, and even the planet.

A Cosmic Dynamo is the activation of the center of movement of a sacred place, such as a mountain or a stone circle, through physical human activity, ceremony, intention, and offerings. As with the power of prayer, the Cosmic Dynamo allows each tiny human being to have a positive influence on others, by radiating outward, first personal, then social intentions to the community. This force is exponentially increased when people join their energy together with the Earth forces to manifest whatever is on the agenda for that day.

I have been studying for three years with a brilliant and eloquent Aztec/Toltec teacher, Sergio Magaña Ocelocoyotl (coyote jaguar), and his teachers, as mentioned in the previous story.

The Cosmic Dynamo

When they're not leading ceremony, Xolotl and Alma (as well as Sergio) share their Mexica cosmovision and wisdom with eager students. One of the most memorable concepts that they both taught was that of this Cosmic Dynamo.

In one of Alma's teaching sessions, she described the healing nature of ceremonial dancing, as we did on the Solstice. Participants place an intention along with a photo, or other personal item on the altar at the center of the dance. The movement creates a vortex of energy, and the focus of the dancers' intentions sends the healing to its destination, be it personal or planetary. Ceremonial dancing creates the *ollin*, the movement that feeds the Earth chakra (in the case of the Solstice, the *Zocalo*, an energetic epicenter of Mexico City) which, in turn, powers the Cosmic Dynamo.

Through the intricate and beautiful altar that centered our Solstice ceremony, I felt the group raise a powerful vortex. As it grew more expansive and rose to the heavens, I felt myself doing the same. Much later, when I returned to my hotel, I fell into dreams of jaguars and serpents racing through my blood and native dancers executing perfect hummingbird steps. Upon waking, I realized I was once again a believer…in the magic and mystery of the universe, something I often lose touch with, wrapped up in the little day-to-day issues of life. I also felt I had an indigenous piece of the "wild" now planted within me that I could access in the future, when needed. A cure for my often over-civilized modern life. As a visual artist, I also felt gifted with an abundance of raw, new, archetypal material.

Bonus Story - The Cosmic Dynamo

The Cosmic Dynamo and Cultural Comparisons

I've spun Tibetan prayer wheels; never quite believing that a simple mechanical action could actually send supplications into the ether.

I've walked labyrinths, where physical movement took me on both an inner and outer journey to a still center. But it was always a solo process. Never for the community. Imagine going into a labyrinth with intentions and having them radiate to the world upon the out-spiraling!

In Wiccan rituals, I've joined and led groups in setting a healing intention; raising a cone of power and sending the energy off to a person, community, or the planet. *Anchoring and amplifying* the power through a vibrational epicenter of the Earth takes this to a very different level. **When you create a Cosmic Dynamo you're activating an Earth chakra.** You're invoking it to work with you.

In the case of the Solstice, we activated a sacred, ceremonial site. When that Earth chakra is a mountain, what's activated is the mountain's heart: its cave. We also activate our own inner cave (*chicomostoc*) or shadow, in this system, transforming the unknown, the enemy into our Higher Self—the hero who is ready to help the collective. *We have within us a portal to a place of great power.*

Bonus Story - The Cosmic Dynamo

How to Move a Mountain

The bus emerged from the diesel-fumed crush of the city. Closer and closer we sped toward a snow-capped mountain. After our lesson on activating Earth chakras, I was eager to put theory into practice. But the mountain we were approaching was puffing out white clouds like a steam engine! I recognized it as one of the two sacred volcanoes of Mexico City—Popocatepetl. This Earth chakra already seemed quite active without any human assistance! Would we be working here? My palms started to sweat...

The heart of a mountain (and any organism) is the center of its movement. According to Xolotl, "In our (Nahuatl) cosmovision, everything has a (vibrational) center. Therefore when we activate sacred things, when we activate the sacred mountains, what we offer is directed to all."

A thin bowl of a moon hung slightly over the horizon, echoing the shape of the volcanic crater where we would perform ceremony. An arduous climb up a steep, slippery, shale-covered slope turned the group not inward, but outward toward helping each other as physical limitations were keenly felt. At the summit, we were truly humble warriors, bonded closely with the volcano Cuicuilco. The equally hair-raising and steep descent into the cave of its caldera brought new sensations: cold, pervasive dampness, but also the feeling of being in the sacred womb of the Earth mother, where we could almost hear her breathing.

Just like at the Zocalo, the altar was strewn with offerings including flowers and sacred sweets called tzoalli, *made from chocolate, amaranth, tequila and honey. The* tzoalli *were arranged in a wheel, representing movement (ollin) and became the center of the Cosmic Dynamo. The ceremony in the cave was quick, because of the extreme discomfort of the location, but, as many later realized, most effective.*

~

Bonus Story - The Cosmic Dynamo

Sergio says, "We persist…in wanting to remain exactly the same, regardless of the perpetual movement and unaware of all the changes that occur on a constant basis…", and that as humans, we have an inherent tendency to fall into weakness: "the part that in this eternal renewal process prevents us from gaining access to a new idea of ourselves and to its manifestation."

~

"The human experience is constant change," says Xolotl. To remain aware, "we need to create our *own* change regularly to counteract our separation from pure essence."

Ometeotl. (And so it is!)

Bonus Story - The Cosmic Dynamo

Reviews are precious (and very helpful) to us! We would be so very grateful if you took a moment to leave us a review on the Amazon.com page for *The Secret of the Cylinder*. The URL will be this:

http://www.amazon.com/Secret-Cylinder-Book-Sekhmet/dp/0975520725

If you search for the book title or author name, it will come up too.

Thank you!!!

Michele Fontaine and Wadjet Publishing

The Secret of the Cylinder

Other Titles by Wadjet Publishing:

Harem Sister

A young woman's quest for personal power in ancient Persia
(Book 1 of the Sekhmet Series)
Michele Fontaine

A past-life tale set in the Persian Empire of 500 BC, *Harem Sister* takes you from incense-strung bazaars to the belly-dance tents of Shiraz and the coriander-steeped kitchens of Basra. Kidnapped from her privileged childhood home and sold to a harem, Amat faces challenges that transform her into a wise young woman in her struggle for freedom.

The Secret of the Cylinder

A tarot reading reveals danger if she does not heed the wisdom of new allies. Befriended by Esmet, harem elder and former priestess of Isis, and Kamal, a 10-year-old slave boy who has the key to Amat's freedom, she finds the friendship and counsel that she needs. Will she heed the wisdom of the prophecy? And will it take the power of the old Gods and Goddesses of Egypt to grant her the freedom she so dearly seeks?

ISBN 978-0-615-12146-8

192 pages

"Set in the Persian Empire of 500 B.C. *Harem Sister* is the story of Amat, a woman beset by challenges. When Amat's family is killed and she is drawn into the deceptive pleasures of harem life, she must heed warnings and wisdom to find the self-determination and wherewithal to live her own life. A strong and sensual tale of will and resolve, *Harem Sister* is an original novel which is based in part upon a past-life experience of the author and so will be of especial interest for students of past-life regression and metaphysical studies." ~ Midwest Book Review

"A flame of poetry!" ~ Cerridwen Fallingstar, author of *The Heart of the Fire and White as Bone, Red as Blood*

"Lovely and evocative descriptions of the dancing and of harem life!" ~ Michelle Richmond, author of *The Year of Fog*

"You have a strong and powerful spirit! May the rising spirit in you heal many broken spirits." ~ Sobonfu Some, author of *The Spirit of Intimacy*

Fire of Isis

The Forbidden Temple of Basra

(Book 2 of the Sekhmet Series)

Michele Fontaine

Fire of Isis continues our tale of Kamal, beautiful slave boy and healer, who became Amat's "adopted" brother in *Harem Sister*. Free at last from his second pleasure prison with Hassan, the infatuated former Harem Keeper who stole him from the sheik of Shiraz, Kamal is driven to discover Amat's fate. His search takes him to Basra, where he finds Esmet, who was once his harem elder. And the Forbidden Temple.

The Secret of the Cylinder

In a land hostile to the ancient gods and goddesses of Egypt, Isis' two priestesses built a temple. Esmet and Anath, once courtesans, now lovers, enjoy the protection of Belshazaar, king of Basra, and former betrothed of Amat. But their security is threatened by Kamal's appearance. Upon learning of Amat's death, Kamal begins a tormented journey to Egypt, where, impossibly, he finds her — but in a new body, and in grave peril. Can Kamal save Amat, (now Meresankh — she who loves life) from her new captivity? And will his very own son be the downfall of the Desert Priestesses of Isis and their Forbidden Temple?

ISBN 978-0-9755207-0-3

164 pages

"I really have enjoyed this series. It is an easy, cozy up to a fire with a warm blanket story. I love the historical background, the exotic descriptions and the mystical references. The descriptions of sacred ritual interwoven into the story are very filling for me.

I would highly recommend book 1 - *Harem Sister*, before reading this one, they really do go together. Michele does a good job of retelling important parts of the story so that if you don't read it, it's o.k. but it would be a much better reading experience if you had read #1 first." ~ Kirsten Sahagun

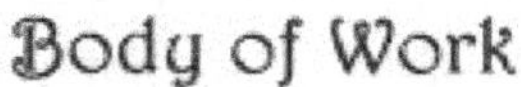

Body of Work

Short Stories. Tall Tales. Inspiration.

Michele Fontaine

This collection of short stories spans 30 years of inner and outer exploration . . . of exotic places, spiritual spaces, and soul-searing embraces. It's *Eat, Pray Love* meets *Water for Elephants*, with quirky characters peppering the plots and calling the shots from Ubud to Udine.

Encompassing ten years of writing, *Body of Work* contains some pieces previously published in the San Francisco Chronicle, Travelers' Tales, and Shamans Drum Magazine; and other stories seeing the light of day for the first time in this book. *Body of Work*'s stories are grouped into Food, Spiritual Travel, Love/Death, and Remembrance/Transformation.

Mostly autobiographical, at times experimental, hilarious, introspective and wise, *Body of Work* takes the reader running with the author on a near-marital workout in Cusco, Peru; through the gauntlet of snapping wild hounds at sunrise in Ubud, Bali; and literally off a runway in her modeling days in Boston. Through it all, author Michele Fontaine manages to find a humble place in the universe, a connection with all of humanity, and a good laugh.

Follow Michele on her day and a half working for author Danielle Steele . . . her big night out at Studio 54 in the 1980's . . . sweet memories of her mother's spring cleaning rituals in the 1960's.

With self-deprecating humor, loving detail about a mother's memory, and an ability to turn even a chocolate addiction into a life lesson, Michele takes pen in hand again to gently, laughingly, achingly, and sometimes slyly and passionately explore the depths of humanness.

ISBN 978-0-9755207-1-0

232 pages

And a sneak peek at Wadjet Publishing's next title:

Body of Work 2

Short Stories. Tall Tales. Inspiration.

Michele Fontaine

A new series of adventures on the road and into the mystery....

Featuring Chapter 1 - Cirque Microsaurus

The Secret of the Cylinder

And a sneak peek at Wadjet Publishing's next title:

Cirque Microsaurus

The 86-foot wing-sail catamaran bobbed gently at Pier 27. An obsidian missile, the AC72 pranced in place with trophy-winning elegance, with each exhale of the waves. Equally elegant were the 20 models milling at the end of the dock, shivering slightly, but breathtaking nonetheless in matching black vinyl monokinis. Carrie Livingston surveyed the crowning glory of her lifetime achievement, then the goosebumped legion. She inhaled deeply, and accepted a glass of champagne from a tuxedoed waiter.

"I love the Bay in May," she purred.

"Those poor, cold girls," piped her equally stunning partner, Pandora — graceful fingers twining around a flute of Cristal. Her black pleather minidress hugged her luscious curves, as she tugged on a smart leather jacket, shivering.

Noticing the frown playing on Pandora's features, Carrie smiled. "Don't worry, darling…they're just for our inspiration," she whispered into her lover's ear. "You're my only and my everything." Carrie took Pandora's left hand and kissed it; lips brushing the green diamond she'd given her on their wedding day. They both sported the same $10K hammered gold band from Pavé in Berkeley, set with a glittering five-carat stone.

One of the models strode up to the couple.

"Ah, Mona Middleton, my QA lead," exclaimed Carrie, as she wrapped her arm around Mona's shoulders, causing Pandora's creamy forehead to crinkle once again.

"Pandora, sweetie, please meet my most valuable employee, and one of the most brilliant minds at Soothsayer. Mona, Pandora used to be a top hacker and debugger…the latter for me…but of course, now, she's otherwise occupied."

Pandora forced a smile as she shook the girl's blue hand.

"Ms. Livingston, I am so thrilled to be part of your team…and THIS team" she waved towards the other girls. Your enlightened management is as successful as I know this beautiful vessel will be. I just wanted to congratulate you and say thanks!"

"Thank you, dear. Now, why don't you take this glass of champagne, and make sure the rest of the girls have one too."

 Carrie motioned to a beefcake waiter, who was hovering nearby. On cue, a radio announcer from KNBR/ESPN Radio picked up a microphone and faced the crowd. "Welcome everybody! On this auspicious day, we celebrate and inaugurate the maiden voyage of Silicon Valley superstar Carrie Livingston's racing catamaran, Soothsayer II. A contender for the America's Cup Championship in 2016, it's 86 feet long, carries a crew of 11, and is able to reach speeds of 88 mph. Carrie, if you'll do the honors…"

The announcer picked up a champagne bottle from the tiny, black velvet-draped table before him and handed it to Carrie. Sizing up the bobbing hull, she took a wide stance with her stilettos and swung the bottle like a baseball bat. It shattered with an epic crack. The punt flew toward her, whacking her head with a noticeable thunk.

Cirque Microsaurus

She fell like a K.O.'d prizefighter; her coconut making a sickening hollow sound as it hit the wharf. And then she lay motionless.

Pandora rushed over, "Someone call 911!" she shrieked.

The media surged past the horrified and shivering models. Not missing a beat, the announcer continued his live narration: "Ms. Livingston is DOWN! In a tragic turn of events, as she was christened her catamaran, IT mogul Carrie Livingston has been struck down by the punt of the very champagne bottle she was swinging…"

Flashbulbs exploded and the audience gasped.

"Known to be a bit on the eccentric side — requiring of all her employees mandatory onsite daily yoga and meditation — Ms. Livingston is nonetheless regarded as the most successful tech mogul in Silicon Valley; with Soothsayer earnings for fiscal 2013 topping 17.6 billion. Thought to be at the top of her game, Ms. Livingston — at 55 years old — has everything to live for."

Sirens approached, as the chattering, confused models huddled like Emperor penguins that had just lost their egg. Some of the more enterprising paparazzi offered them their jackets.

~

Word spread like wildfire at Soothsayer headquarters. As the announcement rippled through the building, incredulous employees prairie-dogged over their cubicle walls and conjectured heatedly at the Smoothie Bar.

"Is she still in a coma?" a bloom-cheeked geek wondered, wide-eyed, over his Monster Mango-rama with protein powder. "What does this mean for all of us?"

Cirque Microsaurus

"What if she doesn't make it?" another posited, slurping the last of his Banana Mamma Jamma. "This blows, dude."

Bets were placed on whether she would live or die at what Forbes magazine called "the most enlightened workplace in Silicon Valley".

~

Beep…beep…beep…*What's that annoying sound?* Carrie slowly opened her eyes. She saw nothing but white mist. *Am I dead?* she wondered, blinking. Slowly a hospital room came into focus…and the face of a beautiful woman in a black leather jacket peering down at her.

"Who are *you*?" Carrie asked, frowning.

Pandora's naked left hand flew to her mouth.

"Short term memory loss is common after a concussion and coma," the doctor had assured her. "Since she's physically fine, why don't you take her home and try to jog her memory. That would be the best treatment at this point."

~

Carrie stepped into her Woodside mansion gingerly, eyeing everything as if for the first time. Pandora squeezed Carrie's ringless left hand, "Does anything look familiar, sweetie?"

Shaking her head, Carrie let herself be led on a tour. As they entered the master bedroom, she took in all 1200 square feet of it. Nearly snow blind from the pure whiteness of its swath of carpet, white furniture, and comforter, she approached the custom Duxiana with a frown.

Cirque Microsaurus

"What are all those stuffed dinosaurs doing on the bed?" she puzzled.

"Sweetie, these are all yours! Actually, I've been hoping for the past year that you'd grow tired of them, but you said you had one as a little girl. The decorator thinks they're a nightmare, but they make you so happy... No, huh?"

"Nope. Sorry." Carrie sat on the bed weakly, cradling a 10-inch sauropod.

~

Over the next several weeks, the *froideur* between Carrie and Pandora grew steadily worse. All of Pandora's loving efforts at rekindling Carrie's memories as well as their relationship, failed. Finally, Carrie asked Pandora to move out...that she needed time alone to sort out who she was now, since it seemed her old self wasn't returning.

"Since we're not married, this will all be much easier, right?" she said to Pandora's retreating back. The front door slammed. Carrie was alone at last.

Over the next few weeks of solitude and soul-searching, Carrie realized she had lost all interest in sailing, in her business, and in women. She kept hoping something would resonate...an interest, an idea...anything.

Facing her white laptop in her white bedroom one night, it hit her. On her screen was the home page of an unusual business just south of Tuvalu...

~

Cirque Microsaurus

"Ultimate Exotic Pet," a Kiwi-accented voice replied, "We fulfill your extreme animal needs."

Eyebrows raised, Carrie pulled the cell phone from her ear and stared at it, then shrugged.

"I'd like to set up a visit."

~

In the two weeks before her trip to the South Pacific, she made the city of San Francisco an offer they couldn't refuse, and bought Candlestick Park. Workers began retrofitting it to become an enclosed tropical jungle.

She then proceeded to kit out her private 767 jet with 20 spacious cages. "Just keep the animals separate from the main cabin, she told the engineers. "I don't want to smell the poop."

~

The tall, musclebound Kiwi led her down a jungle path. Carrie found herself staring at his bulging biceps, then brought her gaze up to his eyes.

"So you want to create a…"

"Circus."

"You know these are mostly reptiles, ma'am…they're not very bright. Except for the Pakicetus. It's the doglike ancestor to the whale. And Phosphatherium, the pig-sized ancestor to the elephant."

"I've made my fortune doing things people said were impossible. Show me what you've got."

Cirque Microsaurus

~

OK, so that'll be two Microraptors, two Raptorex, five Microceratops, three Nemicolopteri, two Phosphatherium, and two Pakicetus...oh yes, and three of the smallest Velociraptors. Next I need to give you their care and dietary requirements...

"Tell me, Aidan, has anyone ever tried to train these creatures?"

"Actually yes, let me show you what Pakicetus can do..." (They approached a fenced area.) "Here boy, fetch!" Aidan tossed a ball to the far end of the cage, and Paki raced after it, catching it midair on a bounce. The russet, doglike creature returned with the ball, dropped it to the ground, and sat, gazing at Aidan and Carrie with intelligent, blue eyes. Then Aiden threw it a beach ball and Paki bounced it on his nose several times. "Good boy!"

Carrie clapped and laughed, causing Paki to scurry away to a corner and hide.

"We'll have to work on the applause thing," Aidan shrugged.

~

"So who's going to care for them in San Francisco?" Aiden asked. "Actually, if they could spare you here, I'd like to bring you with," Carrie grinned. "How does $250K/year sound?"

"Good as gold, mate."

~

Aiden's leg casually brushed against Carries in the jet cabin. Shivers ran up her spine and she nearly spilled her Chateau Margeaux on the white carpet. "Of course, I'll hire you as many

169

assistants as you need," she said, recovering. "Now this isn't going to be a zoo! Carrie waved a caviar-laden cracker in emphasis. "I don't want the animals to be gawked at until showtime! Until I say so! I want full creative control here…"

"I'll do my best, ma'am," Aiden replied, patting her knee, and causing some precious drops of Margeaux to pattern the carpet this time.

~

Practice began, with a few missing fingers among the handsomely paid-off workers.

As training ensued and the Park's media kit began to circulate, Carrie found she had a three ring circus sooner than expected…When the media began spotting Carrie and Aiden at the swankiest restaurants in San Francisco, and his car parked by her house nightly.

Someone else noticed the nocturnal visits. "She thinks she can just throw me away…" Pandora muttered from the neighbor's hedge.

~

Finally it was opening night for Cirque Microsaurus…Thousands of expectant children, parents and media clogged the 101. Private shuttles, boats and helicopters turned out to be the most successful method of gaining entry to the sold-out arena.

The show began with the paki's doggy tricks, the wonder of the four-winged flyers, and the sweetness of the pig-sized elephant. This was followed by wild dancing by the foot-tall Microceratops, who waggled their ruffs comically and made the audience laugh as they danced to the Nutcracker Suite.

Cirque Microsaurus

The T Rexes and velociraptors followed, wowing the audience as they chased balls, Aiden, and each other, in a somewhat synchronized manner.

As the grand finale ensued, Carrie stood proudly in the center of the floor, white top hat and tails matching Aiden's. Just as the music crescendoed, the stadium was plunged into darkness. Screams pierced the gloom. Then there was the crunch of huge metal doors being wrenched open. Chill bay gusts ripped through the stadium.

Not far from a nearby P.E. & E. transformer that she'd hacked and shut down, Pandora cackled evilly. "You think you can love cold blooded creatures, Ms. Livingston? How about a bunch of dead reptiles?!"

~

Pandemonium ensued, as animals and humans run helter skelter. One particularly oversized Velociraptor slammed full tilt into a tent support beam near Carrie. It cracked and began falling in slow motion. As the deathly fog swirled into her tropical Thunderdome, and her little denizens began dying, Carrie screamed, but found she couldn't make a sound. The beam bonked her on the head and she blacked out, as the pakis and tiny elephants rush to their fallen mother's side, huddling for warmth and safety.

~

Carrie woke in a hospital room, panting, with a loving Pandora pressing her favorite stuffed dino to her. "My babies!" She gasped, eyes wild and unfocused, then gradually resting on Pandora.

"Your babies are right here and they're fine," Pandora soothed.

"But the circus?! Aiden?!...Was it YOU that killed them all?" she snapped.

Pandora looked puzzled...then horrified. She took a deep breath and unfurrowed her forehead.

"You've been in a coma for two weeks, sweetie. You suffered a concussion when you were hit in the head by the punt of the champagne bottle you christened Soothsayer II with. Do you remember?"

Slowly, thoughtfully, Carrie began nodding.

It had all been a dream.

Carrie began to laugh, as she took Pandora's hand. She noticed that the green diamond set into the hammered gold band that she'd given her on their wedding day was still there.

Carrie grabbed her favorite stuffed dinosaur, which lay next to her on her bed and threw it into the wastebasket across the room.

"Come here, baby," Carrie said as she pulled Pandora to her and tipped her face up.

Pandora drew the privacy curtain with a secret smile, and kissed her resurrected lover.

Catalog – Ultimate Exotic Pet

"We fulfill all your extreme animal needs."

1. Smallest Tyrannosaur – Raptorex

The king of all dinosaurs, Tyrannosaurus Rex, measured about 40 feet from head to tail and weighed 7 or 8 tons—but its fellow tyrannosaur Raptorex, which lived about 60 million years earlier, tipped the scales at 150 pounds, max, an object lesson in how plus-sized creatures evolve from wee ancestors. Raptorex hails from northwest China and is considered the prototype for T Rex.

2. Smallest Ceratopsian - Microceratops

Microceratops (also known as Microceratus), (Compsognathus longipes) the smallest of all the ceratopsian ("horn-faced") dinosaurs, was only about a foot and a half high and weighed all of four or five pounds. Unlike its much larger cousins — such as Triceratops and Pentaceratops — Microceratops scooted around on two feet, which probably helped it to avoid getting stomped on by bigger dinosaurs. Its closest relative was the slightly bigger Psittacosaurus, which is famous for being one of the few dinosaurs to have been eaten by Mesozoic mammals, rather than the other way around! The smallest known dinosaur, Compsognathus was about the size of a chicken.

3. Smallest Elephant - Phosphatherium

Phosphatherium popped up in the fossil record only about 5 million years after the dinosaurs went extinct, and if you didn't know where it fit on the mammalian evolutionary tree, you wouldn't know whether this three-foot-long, 100-pound herbivore was fated to become a pig, a hippo, or a prehistoric elephant. It turns out that the last guess is the right one: modern elephants, as well as Ice Age Mastodons and Mammoths, can trace their family tree back to this squat, ungainly creature.

4. Smallest Whale – Pakicetus

The ultimate ancestor of modern whales was the early Eocene Pakicetus, a small, inoffensive, furry mammal that only weighed about 50 pounds (or as much as a second-grader). Interestingly, Pakicetus was a land-dwelling, four-footed animal similar in appearance to a modern dog; we only know to classify it as a prehistoric whale because of the characteristic structure of its inner ears.

© 2012 Encyclopædia Britannica, Inc.

5. Velociraptor Mongoliensis

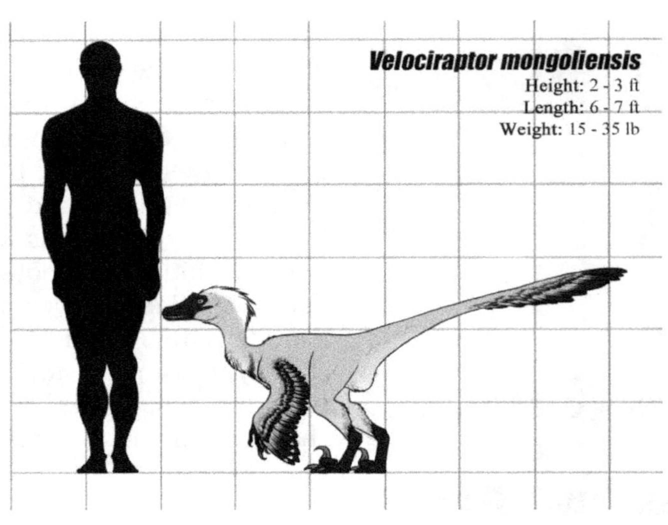

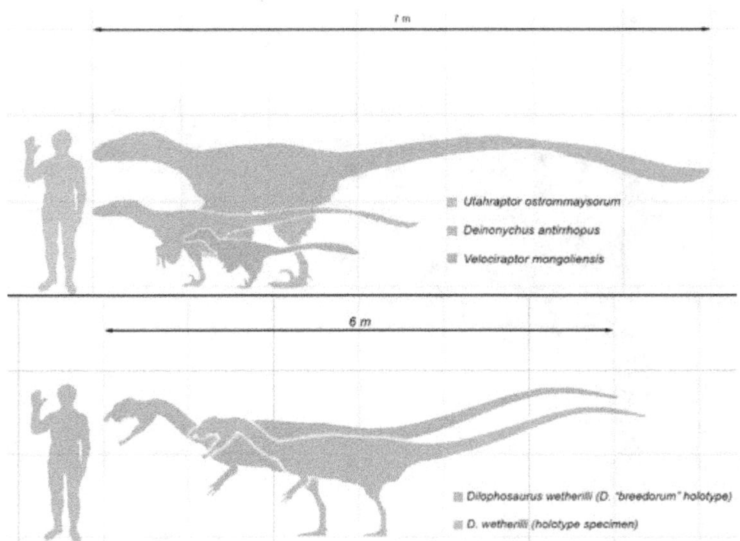

6. Smallest Pterosaur - Nemicolopterus

A couple of years ago, it seemed that the remains of new pterosaurs were being dug up in China every week. In February of 2008, paleontologists discovered the fossil of Nemicolopterus, the smallest pterosaur yet identified, which had a wingspan of only 10 inches and weighed a few ounces. Oddly enough, this pigeon-sized reptile may have occupied the same branch of pterosaur evolution that gave rise to the enormous Quetzalcoatlus 50 million years later.

7. Smallest Raptor - Microraptor

With its feathers and four, count 'em, four primitive wings (one set each on its forearms and hind legs), the early Cretaceous Microraptor might easily have been mistaken for a bizarrely mutated pigeon. This was, however, a genuine raptor, albeit one that only measured about two feet from head to tail and weighed a few pounds soaking wet. Befitting its tiny size, paleontologists believe that Microraptor subsisted on a diet of insects.

Catalog - Ultimate Exotic Pet

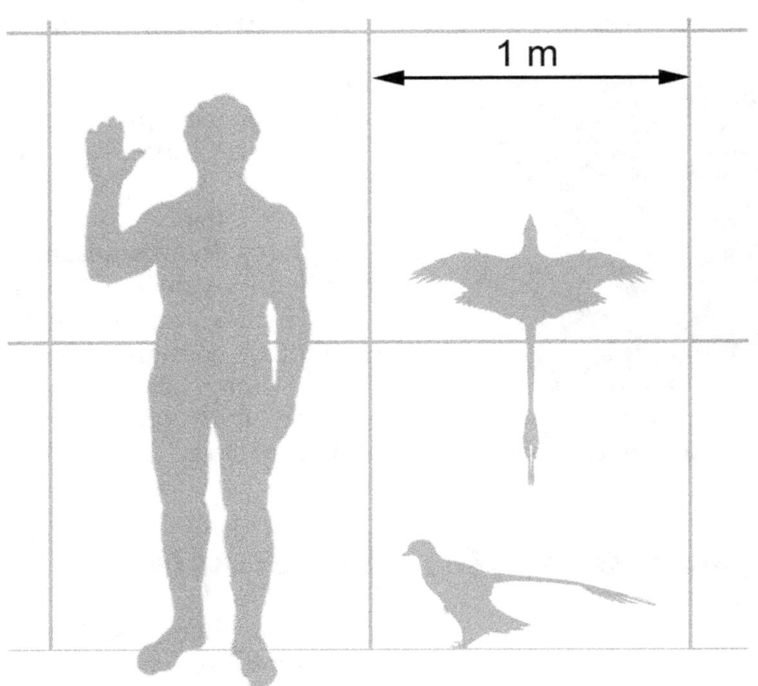

Sources:

Image1 - "Raptorex SIZE 01" by Conty - Own work. Licensed under CC BY 3.0 via Commons - https://commons.wikimedia.org/wiki/File:Raptorex_SIZE_01.jpg#/media/File:Raptorex_SIZE_01.jpg

Image 2 - http://dinosaurs.about.com/od/carnivorousdinosaurs/p/raptorex.htm

Image 3 - http://dinopedia.wikia.com/wiki/Microceratus

Image 4: http://www.hominides.com/data/images/illus/Exposition_mammouths/phosphatherium.jpg

 Image 5: "Pakicetus SIZE" by Conty - Own work. Licensed under CC BY 3.0 via Commons - https://commons.wikimedia.org/wiki/File:Pakicetus_SIZE.png#/media/File:Pakicetus_SIZE.png

Image 6: https://allyouneedisbiology.files.wordpress.com/2015/
09/143519-004-b19ffd4e.jpg **also** https://
allyouneedisbiology.wordpress.com/category/marine-
mammals/
Image 7: https://www.weasyl.com/submission/55349/
velociraptor-mongoliensis
Image 8: http://paleoillustration.tumblr.com/page/36
Image 9: http://dinosaurs.about.com/od/aviandinosaurs3/p/
nemicolopterus.htm
Image 10: https://en.wikipedia.org/wiki/Microraptor
Image 11: http://www.dinosaurfarm.com/wp-content/uploads/
2013/11/Microraptor-Carnegie1.jpg

http://dinosaurs.about.com/od/typesofdinosaurs/tp/Five-
Smallest-Dinosaurs.htm

www.ingramcontent.com/pod-product-compliance
Lightning Source LLC
Chambersburg PA
CBHW070031120726
47909CB00003B/1125

* 9 7 8 0 9 7 5 5 2 0 7 2 7 *